Collection One

CLEMENTINE ROSE

Books by Jacqueline Harvey

Clementine Rose and the Surprise Visitor
Clementine Rose and the Pet Day Disaster
Clementine Rose and the Perfect Present
Clementine Rose and the Farm Fiasco
Clementine Rose and the Seaside Escape
Clementine Rose and the Treasure Box
Clementine Rose and the Famous Friend
Clementine Rose and the Ballet Break-In
Clementine Rose and the Movie Magic
Clementine Rose and the Birthday Emergency
Clementine Rose and the Special Promise
Clementine Rose and the Paris Puzzle
Clementine Rose and the Wedding Wobbles

Alice-Miranda at School
Alice-Miranda on Holiday
Alice-Miranda Takes the Lead
Alice-Miranda at Sea
Alice-Miranda in New York
Alice-Miranda Shows the Way
Alice-Miranda in Paris
Alice-Miranda Shines Bright
Alice-Miranda in Japan
Alice-Miranda at Camp
Alice-Miranda at the Palace
Alice-Miranda in the Alps
Alice-Miranda to the Rescue
Alice-Miranda in China
Alice-Miranda Holds the Key
Alice-Miranda in Hollywood

Collection One

CLEMENTINE ROSE

Jacqueline Harvey

RANDOM HOUSE AUSTRALIA

A Random House book
Published by Penguin Random House Australia Pty Ltd
Level 3, 100 Pacific Highway, North Sydney NSW 2060
www.penguin.com.au

Penguin
Random House
Australia

Clementine Rose and the Surprise Visitor first published by
Random House Australia in 2012
Clementine Rose and the Pet Day Disaster first published by
Random House Australia in 2013
Clementine Rose and the Perfect Present first published by
Random House Australia in 2013
This omnibus edition first published by Random House Australia in 2017

Addresses for the Penguin Random House group of companies can be
found at global.penguinrandomhouse.com/offices.

National Library of Australia
Cataloguing-in-Publication entry

Author: Harvey, Jacqueline
Title: Clementine Rose: collection one/Jacqueline Harvey
ISBN: 978 0 14378 864 5 (pbk)
Series: Harvey, Jacqueline. Clementine Rose.
Target audience: For primary school age
Subjects: Girls – Juvenile fiction

Cover and internal illustrations by J.Yi
Cover design by Leanne Beattie
Internal design by Midland Typesetters
Typeset in ITC Century 12.5/19 by Midland Typesetters, Australia
Printed in Australia by Griffin Press, an accredited ISO AS/NZS
14001:2004 Environmental Management System printer

Penguin Random House Australia uses papers that are natural,
renewable and recyclable products and made from wood grown
in sustainable forests. The logging and manufacturing processes
are expected to conform to the environmental regulations of the
country of origin.

CLEMENTINE ROSE

and the Surprise Visitor

Jacqueline Harvey

RANDOM HOUSE AUSTRALIA

*For Linsay and Julie, who helped dream
her up, and for Ian, as always*

DINNER ROLLS

Clementine Rose was delivered not in the usual way, at a hospital, but in the back of a mini-van, in a basket of dinner rolls. There was no sign of any mother or father.

Pierre Rousseau, the village baker, had made several stops that morning before his last call at the crumbling mansion known as Penberthy House, on the edge of the village of Penberthy Floss. As Pierre's van skidded to a halt on the gravel drive at the back door, he thought he heard a faint meowing sound.

'Claws, that better not be you back there,' Pierre grouched. He wondered if he had yet again managed to pick up Mrs Mogg's cheeky tabby when he stopped to make his delivery at the general store. Claws had a habit of sneaking on board when Pierre wasn't looking and had often taken the trip around the village with him.

But Claws did not reply.

Pierre hopped out of the van and walked around to the side door. A faded sign in swirly writing said 'Pierre's Patisserie – cakes and pastries of distinction'. He grabbed the handle and slid open the panel.

'Good morning, Pierre,' a voice called from behind him.

'Good morning, Monsieur Digby,' Pierre called back. 'You must 'ave a full 'ouse this weekend, *non*?'

'No, Lady Clarissa just likes to be prepared in case there's a last-minute rush,' said Digby.

But there never *was* a last-minute rush. Digby Pertwhistle had been the butler at Penberthy House for almost fifty years. He had started working for Lord and Lady Appleby as a young man and when they both passed away over twenty years ago their only child, Lady Clarissa, had taken charge. Digby loved Lady Clarissa like a daughter.

As well as the house, Lady Clarissa had inherited a small sum of money from her parents. But Penberthy House had sixty rooms and a roof that leaked in at least sixty places. Soon the money had all been spent and there were still more repairs to be done. So to help pay the bills, Lady Clarissa had opened the house to guests as a country hotel. Unfortunately, business wasn't exactly booming. Penberthy Floss was a very pretty village but it was a little out of the way.

Although Lady Clarissa didn't always have the best of luck with the house, she had the most incredible good fortune with competitions. It had started years ago when she was just ild. With her mother's help she had sent ... an entry to the newspaper to win a pony. Three days before her ninth birthday, a letter had arrived to say that she was the winner of a shaggy Shetland, which she called Princess Tiggy. Her love of contests had continued and everyone in the village knew of Lady Clarissa's winning ways. Mrs Mogg would put aside newspapers and magazines and make sure that she marked all of the competitions available.

Over the years, Lady Clarissa had won lots of different things that helped her keep the house running. There were electrical appliances, a kitchen makeover and even several holidays which she gave to Mr Pertwhistle in return for his hard work. She often gave prizes she didn't need to her friends in the village too. They frequently protested and said that she should sell her winnings and pay for the upkeep of the house, but Lady Clarissa would have none of it. If Penberthy House was a little chilly from time to time, or they had to keep a good supply of buckets to set around the place whenever it rained, it didn't matter. Just as long as the people she cared about had everything they needed.

But that's all quite beside the point. This morning there was a delivery that would change Lady Clarissa's life more than any prize could.

Pierre Rousseau and Digby Pertwhistle were standing beside the delivery van chatting about the weather when Pierre put his fore-finger to his lips.

'Shhh, did you 'ear that?' he whispered.

'What?' Digby replied. The old man cocked his head and frowned.

'That noise, like a kitten,' Pierre explained.

'No, I don't hear anything but I'd better take those rolls and get a move on,' Digby said as he glanced into the van. They were enter-taining three guests that evening. It wasn't exactly a full house, but more visitors than in the past few weekends. Perhaps things were looking up.

Digby pulled the basket towards him. He

picked it up from the edge of the van and staggered under the weight.

'Good grief, man! What did you put in these rolls? Bricks?' Digby exclaimed.

'What do you mean?' asked Pierre, looking shocked.

Digby Pertwhistle handed him the basket and Pierre strained under the unexpected weight. '*Sacré bleu!* My rolls are as light as a feather. That rotten Claws, he must be 'iding in the bottom of this basket. My bread will be ruined.'

Pierre lifted the tea towel that was covering the rolls.

His mouth fell open. He looked, then gently put the basket back down in the van, rubbed his eyes and looked again.

Digby Pertwhistle looked too.

Both men stared at each other and then at the basket. Fresh white dinner rolls surrounded a tiny face with rose-pink lips and bright blue eyes.

Pierre finally found his voice. 'That's not Claws. It's a baby.'

'It's a baby, all right,' Digby agreed. 'But where did it come from? And more importantly, who does it belong to?'

Pierre reached into the basket and gently lifted the infant out. It was dressed in a pink jumpsuit and had a fluffy white blanket around it. Pinned to the blanket was an envelope addressed to Lady Clarissa Appleby, Penberthy House.

'It's not my usual delivery,' Pierre said. 'But it is meant for Lady Clarissa.'

'How did the baby get into the van?' Digby Pertwhistle wondered out loud.

'It must have been when I was at Mrs Mogg's store,' Pierre replied. 'But I don't remember seeing anyone in the village.'

Cradling the tiny child in his arms, Pierre Rousseau, followed closely by Digby Pertwhistle, made the most important delivery of his life.

Lady Clarissa was in the kitchen up to her elbows in washing up. A newborn baby was the last thing she expected on that sunny spring day. But Lady Clarissa took the child's arrival in her stride, just as she did most things.

The note pinned to the baby's blanket read:

Dear Lady Clarissa,
Her name is Clementine Rose and she is yours. The papers attached to this letter say so. No one can take her from you. Please do not look for me. I came on the wind and now I am gone.
Love her, as I wish I could have done.
E

Pierre suggested they call the police. 'It's not right to find a baby in a basket of dinner rolls,' he declared.

Digby added, 'It's not right to find a baby without a mother.'

But from the moment Lady Clarissa locked eyes with Clementine Rose, a bond was struck. Lady Clarissa was in love. Digby Pertwhistle was too. And the paperwork was all in order.

The old man bustled about the house

finding this and that. He remembered that Lady Clarissa's baby things had been stored years ago in the attic and, without a word of prompting, he set off to find what he could.

Pierre disappeared into the village and returned with a box of baby requirements. He bought nappies and formula and even dummies and bibs. He had two young children of his own. His daughter Sophie was just a month old, so he knew a lot about babies.

'Mrs Mogg, she will come and 'elp tonight with your guests,' he explained.

Clementine Rose gurgled and cooed, she slept and she ate. But she hardly ever cried. It was as if she knew right from that first moment how much she was loved and adored, even though she was far too young to understand it at all. And over the years she grew up and no one could remember what life had been like before that fateful morning she arrived in the basket of dinner rolls.

THE LETTER

Clementine Rose stared at her reflection in the hall mirror. She wrinkled her nose and furrowed her brow and concentrated as hard as she could. She stared and stared, her blue eyes gazing back at her like pools of wet ink. But no matter how long she thought about it, her ears simply would not wiggle.

'How do you do that, Uncle Digby?' Clementine turned around and looked at Digby Pertwhistle as his rather large ears flapped like washing.

'Years of practice,' the old man replied.

'But I practise every time I walk past this mirror,' she said, 'and no matter how hard I try, my ears don't wiggle at all.'

Digby looked at her and smiled. 'You're good at lots of other things, Clemmie.'

'Like getting into trouble,' Clementine replied. 'I'm good at that.'

Digby grinned at her. It was true that the child had a knack for getting into all sorts of scrapes, even when she wasn't trying.

'Clementine, are you up there?' her mother called from the bottom of the stairs. 'I'm going to see Mrs Mogg and collect the mail. Would you like to come?'

'Yes, please,' Clementine called back. 'But I'm still in my pyjamas.'

The telephone rang before Lady Clarissa could reply. She walked over to the hall table and picked up the receiver.

'Good morning, Penberthy House, this is Clarissa,' she said. 'Oh, hello Odette, how are you?'

On hearing that name, Clementine ran halfway down the staircase towards her mother.

'Yes, of course we'd love to have Sophie and Jules. That's fine. No, no guests on Sunday night. It's no problem at all. We'll see you then. Bye,' Clarissa said and hung up.

'Are Sophie and Jules coming?' Clementine called. She was bouncing up and down on the spot like Tigger.

'Yes, on Sunday. Pierre and Odette are going to look at a new van and its hours away. They're going to stay in Downsfordvale for the night.'

Clementine's eyes lit up. Sophie was her best friend and Jules was Sophie's brother, who was two years older.

'I can't wait!' Clementine was already thinking about all the things they could do.

'Well, you'd better run along and get dressed quick smart if you want to come with me to the village, Clemmie. We have some guests arriving this afternoon and I need to get back and make a start on dinner,' her mother instructed.

Clementine skittered back upstairs to the landing.

'And I'd better get on and dust those bedrooms,' said Digby. He turned from the mirror he was polishing and grinned at Clementine. 'We don't want our guests complaining about grubby rooms.'

'No, that's true. There are enough other things they can complain about,' she replied. She was thinking of the previous weekend, when a lady called Mrs Pink ran screaming into the hallway saying there was a snake under her bed. Clementine was in her room on the third floor when she heard the commotion and suddenly remembered that she had been playing in that room the day she lost her giant rubber python. It seemed Mrs Pink had found it and wasn't at all happy about it.

Lady Clarissa had to give the woman three cups of tea and a promise of a reduced charge before she'd go back into the room. Clementine was sent to apologise to Mrs Pink, who spent ten minutes telling her off for being so careless with her things, and then the next hour complaining about her sore feet and her bad back and her creaky bones. Clementine had decided right there and then that getting old was not a very sensible thing to do.

Now Clementine ran off to her bedroom. She had been sick with a cold all week and was looking forward to getting out of the house. And she couldn't wait for Sophie and Jules to come on Sunday too.

'There you are, Lavender.' Clementine found her pet lying in the basket on the floor at the end of her bed. 'We're going to see Mrs Mogg.'

Lavender looked up and grunted.

Clementine thought for a moment about what she would wear and then got dressed as quickly as her fingers would allow. She snapped Lavender's lead onto her collar and together the two of them hurried downstairs to meet her mother.

'Oh, Clemmie, that looks lovely. A little overdressed for collecting the mail, perhaps, but I think Mrs Mogg will be thrilled to see you in it,' Lady Clarissa commented.

Clementine twirled around. 'Mrs Mogg makes the best dresses in the whole world.'

Clementine wore a navy smocked tunic and her favourite red patent Mary Jane shoes. Lavender, her tiny teacup pig, wore a sparkling ruby-red collar, which matched Clementine's shoes perfectly.

Lady Clarissa tucked Clementine's blonde hair behind her ear and re-clipped her red bow.

Lavender squealed.

'And I'm sure that Mrs Mogg will notice how lovely you look in your new collar too, Lavender,' said Lady Clarissa as she reached down and patted the top of the tiny silver pig's head.

No one knew where Clementine got her sense of style but it was there, all right. As a baby she would point at things she liked and wave away anything that she didn't want to wear.

Given the poor state of Lady Clarissa's bank balance, she couldn't afford to buy much for

Clemmie. But dear Mrs Mogg loved to sew and as a result Clementine had a huge wardrobe of clothes to wear for every occasion. The child especially adored dresses and as Mrs Mogg loved to make them for her, it was a match made in heaven.

Clementine held Lavender's lead and the three of them took their usual shortcut into the village. They walked through the field at the back of the garden, over the stone bridge across the stream and finally through the churchyard of St Swithun's, where Father Bob was tending his roses by the fence. His ancient bulldog, Adrian, was fast asleep, snoring, on the steps of the church. In the driveway of the rectory next door, Clementine Rose could see Father Bob's shiny new hatchback gleaming proudly in the sun. Her mother had won the little car but decided that Father Bob had much more use for it than she did.

'Good morning, Lady Clarissa. Good morning, Clementine,' he called. 'And good morning, Lavender,' he said in a funny deep voice.

'Hello Father Bob,' the two called back. Lavender squeaked her hello.

'Your roses are looking magnificent,' Clarissa said.

'Thank you, dear. Just between us,' he said, and tapped his finger to his nose, 'I'm hoping for a win at the Highton Mill flower show, God willing. I seem to lose out to Mr Greening from Highton Hall every year and I think it's about time I took home the cup. That one there,' he said, pointing at a particularly beautiful crimson rose, 'is called William Shakespeare and it might just do it for me.'

Clementine skipped over to the fence and pulled one of the blooms towards her.

'Careful, Clemmie,' her mother called, but it was too late. The stem snapped and the perfect rose fell to the ground.

'Oops!' Clementine exclaimed. 'I'm sorry.'

'It's all right, Clementine,' said Father Bob. He walked over and picked it up. 'It's weeks until the show and that flower would have long been finished. Take it with you.' He handed her the stem.

'I didn't mean to break it,' she replied.

Father Bob waved her away. 'Of course you didn't. It's just a rose, Clementine. Another will grow in its place, my dear.'

The child smiled, even though she wasn't entirely sure she was happy. She hoped that Father Bob was telling the truth when he said he didn't mind.

Clarissa and Clementine said goodbye and together with Lavender they walked out through the stone gateway at the front of the church and across the road to the store. Mrs Mogg's old tabby cat, Claws, was sunning himself on the bench seat on the veranda. Clementine reached down to give him a pat and he purred like a diesel engine. Lavender knew better than to come within the cat's reach, having been scratched on the snout several times before. A bell tinkled as Clarissa opened the shop door.

Clementine leaned over and nuzzled her

neck against Claws's face. She was rewarded with a sandpapery lick on her ear.

'Yuck, Claws, that's revolting.' She wiped her ear, then tied Lavender's lead to the opposite end of the bench. She patted the pig's head and followed her mother into the store. Clementine loved its smells: cold ham, hot pies, musk lollies and most of all Mrs Mogg, who smelt like rose petals and powder.

'Good morning,' chirped Margaret Mogg. She was standing behind the counter carefully placing a batch of fresh scones onto a cake stand. 'And don't you look lovely, young lady,' she said to Clementine.

'It's my favourite,' Clementine replied.

'Well, let me have a proper look at you then.' Mrs Mogg twirled her finger and Clemmie spun around. 'Gorgeous. But I've got another on the go.' She winked as she reached under the counter and pulled out some pink polka dot material. 'What do you think about this, then?'

'I love it!' Clementine exclaimed.

'Margaret, you spoil her,' said Clarissa, shaking her head.

'There's nothing else I'd rather be doing. As long as Clementine is happy to wear my clothes, I'm very happy to make them.'

Margaret Mogg turned away from the counter and pulled a pile of mail out of one of the pigeonholes on the wall behind her. Her general store also housed the post office. Everyone in the village had their own little slot in the wall.

She handed Clarissa a small bundle of letters and retrieved a stack of magazines from under the counter. 'I hope you don't mind, dear, but I started a couple of the crosswords. With Clyde away visiting his mother, I've no one to talk to and it's been rather dull in the evenings. I don't for the life of me know how you finish the whole thing. I can't understand some of those clues at all. I've earmarked all the competitions too.'

Mrs Mogg had also benefitted from Clarissa's good luck. When Mrs Mogg's refrigerator broke down, Lady Clarissa won an entire white goods package, which, having just won a remodelled kitchen for Penberthy House, Clarissa didn't need at all.

Clementine was standing in the far aisle looking at the ribbons Mrs Mogg had recently got into the shop. There was a very pretty pale blue one that she was hoping to add to her collection.

She wandered back to where her mother was sorting through the letters. Clementine noticed that there were lots of the ones with the red writing in the corner. They always seemed to make her mother frown.

Clarissa stopped at one with handwriting that was all swirly and curly.

Margaret Mogg watched from the other side of the counter as Clarissa opened the letter and began to read.

Clarissa caught her breath. 'Oh no.'

'Is everything all right, dear?' Mrs Mogg enquired.

'No, not really. Not at all. Aunt Violet is coming to stay,' Clarissa gulped.

'Oh dear.' Mrs Mogg frowned, recalling all

too well the last time Violet Appleby had visited the village. The woman had run up a hefty bill at the store and left her niece to pay for it.

'Who's Aunt Violet?' Clemmie asked.

'She's your grandfather's sister and she's positively horrid and I rather hoped never to see her again after the last time,' said Clarissa. She was looking very pale.

'Is she on the wall?' Clementine asked, referring to the family portraits that hung all over Penberthy House. She couldn't remember her mother ever mentioning anyone called Violet before.

'Yes, two along from your grandfather, on the stairs,' Clarissa replied.

'Oh, she's beautiful, Mummy!' Clementine exclaimed. 'But I call her Grace because you never told me her name.'

'There is nothing gracious about that woman,' Clarissa muttered under her breath to Mrs Mogg and then glanced down at her daughter. 'And remember, Clemmie, that portrait was painted about fifty years ago.'

Clementine wondered what her mother meant.

'When's she coming?' Mrs Mogg asked.

'According to this letter, she'll be here tomorrow afternoon,' Clarissa said. 'We'd better get home.'

'Why don't you like her, Mummy?' Clementine asked.

'It's complicated,' her mother replied. 'She wasn't always mean. In fact, when I was little she was bags of fun. But there were some unfortunate incidents and her horridness has grown on her, a bit like barnacles.'

Barnacles! Clementine had never seen a person with barnacles. Uncle Digby had shown her barnacles clinging to the side of some boats when they went on a trip to the seaside. And they were all over the pier too. But on people? That sounded terrible.

'Hold on a tick.' Mrs Mogg disappeared through the door behind the counter, which led to the kitchen and the flat behind. 'Take this,' she called, returning with a chocolate sponge cake that was beautifully decorated with fresh strawberries. 'Pierre dropped it in this morning on his way through the village and I don't need a whole sponge to myself.' She patted her round tummy.

'Thank you, Margaret. That's wonderful,' Clarissa said. 'I won't have time to bake a thing this afternoon. Come on, Clemmie, we need to hurry.'

'Is Aunt Violet really covered in seashells?' Clementine asked her mother. She'd been thinking about the barnacles for the last few minutes.

Clarissa looked at her daughter quizzically. 'Whatever do you mean, Clementine?'

'You said that her horridness was like barnacles,' Clementine replied.

'Oh, Clemmie, I didn't mean it like that. It's just an expression. She wasn't always mean but the meanness has built up over the years, a bit like the way barnacles grow on boats and things when they're left in the water too long.' Clarissa smiled tightly and shook her

24

head. 'I didn't mean to frighten you, darling. Aunt Violet may be a lot of things but she's not covered in seashells.'

Phew! Clementine was glad to hear it.

Margaret Mogg smiled at the pair. 'Don't you worry yourself, Clementine. I'm sure Aunt Violet will be perfectly well behaved. And don't fret, dear,' she said, looking at Clarissa. 'If she wants to buy anything this time, it will be cash only.'

Clarissa raised her eyebrows, gathered up the mail and placed it in her basket. Mrs Mogg packaged up the sponge in a cake box and put it into a carry bag.

'Thank you, Margaret,' Clarissa sighed.

'Bye, Mrs Mogg,' Clemmie called as she followed her mother quickly out of the shop. 'Bye, Claws,' she called to the sleeping tabby. 'Come on, Lavender.' She gathered up the lead and the little pig skittered to her feet and followed behind her.

AUNT VIOLET

Clementine had been wondering about Aunt Violet and the unfortunate incidents all afternoon. Maybe her mother had accidentally spilled orange juice on her, like Clementine had on one of the guests at breakfast last week. It wasn't Clemmie's fault that the lady was wearing a white pants-suit, and Clemmie was only trying to help because Uncle Digby was busy in the kitchen. Maybe her mother had accidentally snapped the key in the lock of the bathroom door when Aunt

Violet was in there, as Clementine had done to another guest a few weeks before. That lady wasn't happy at all when Uncle Digby had to climb up a ladder and go through the bathroom window to rescue her.

Clementine loved being a good helper. It was just that sometimes things didn't work out the way she planned. She wondered if her mother had been like that too when she was younger.

On the way home from the village she had asked her mother lots of questions about Aunt Violet. But Lady Clarissa was too lost in her own thoughts to give Clemmie the answers she wanted.

When they got back to the house, two of their guests had already arrived. While her mother and Uncle Digby were busy fussing over them, Clementine was left to play on her own with Lavender. She was practising with her skipping rope on the front lawn and Lavender was munching on some long grass near the stone wall when a shiny red car roared up the driveway. Clementine knew it was an expensive one, too, because it had a big silver star on the bonnet. Uncle Digby was always saying that if he won the lottery he would buy one just like it.

Clementine ran over to say hello. She liked greeting the guests and her mother said that it was important to be friendly and make a good impression. A very thin, tall woman with the most perfect silver bobbed hairdo got out of the car. She wore a stylish lime green pants-suit and Clementine noticed her matching shoes. Her huge sunglasses were round and dark and she didn't take them off.

The woman looked at the house and shuddered.

'Hello,' said Clementine. 'I like your shoes. Are you staying here?'

'Yes,' the woman replied. 'What are *you* doing here?' She raised her glasses to the top of her head and narrowed her dark-blue eyes as she studied the child in her pretty dress.

'I live here,' Clementine replied.

The woman glared at her. 'What do you mean you live here? Since when?'

'Since I came with the dinner rolls,' Clementine answered truthfully.

'Since you came with the dinner rolls! What sort of an answer is that?' the woman scoffed. 'Do you know where the lady of the house is?'

'Well, I'm not really sure because Mummy's been running around taking care of some of the other guests. She's been upset ever since we were in the village this morning and she found out that her Aunt Violet is coming tomorrow. I've never met her. She has a beautiful portrait on the stairs and I talk to her quite a bit, except that I call her Grace because I didn't know her real name. But Mummy says that she's horrid and she's like a barnacle. She must be very old too, I think,' Clementine gabbled.

The woman's eyes seemed to change colour from blue to black right in front of Clementine.

She stared at the child.

She leaned closer.

She pointed one finger right in front of Clementine's nose.

And just as she was about to speak, the front door of the house opened and Lady Clarissa raced out onto the driveway.

'Oh, Aunt Violet, you're early. It's good to see you,' she gushed, kissing the woman on both cheeks.

'Really?' Violet straightened her back and arched her perfectly plucked left eyebrow at Clarissa. 'You're glad to see me? That's not what I've just heard. And I told you I'd be here on Friday.'

Clarissa fingered the letter in her pocket. She knew it said Saturday, but there was no point arguing with Aunt Violet.

Clementine was biting her lip. Sometimes she wished she didn't talk so much.

'Clemmie, come and meet your Great-aunt Violet,' Clarissa instructed.

'Oh, we've met,' Violet snarled. 'But when did you have a baby, Clarissa?'

'But I told you before, Aunt Violet, I came with

the dinner rolls,' said Clementine. She wondered if her great-aunt had a hearing problem.

Clarissa began to explain. 'It's complicated –'

'Of course it's complicated. It's never simple with you, dear, is it? Now, are you going to ask me in or do I have to stand out here for the rest of the afternoon?' asked Violet tightly.

'Of course, Aunt Violet, the kettle's on and I've got a lovely chocolate sponge.' Clarissa turned and frowned at Clementine. Clemmie had never seen her mother like this before. 'This way,' said Clarissa and walked back towards the house.

'I need to get Pharaoh,' Violet snapped. She strode around to the passenger side of the car and opened the door. She pulled out a rectangular black bag, and headed for the front door.

Clementine noticed that the bag had mesh on both ends. 'What's Pharaoh?' she asked, peering into the mesh.

The occupant of the bag hissed.

Clementine recoiled. 'I hope he's not a snake. Mummy hates snakes and last week I got into big trouble for leaving my python in one of the bedrooms.'

'He's a sphynx,' Violet replied. She glared at the little girl. 'And he doesn't like children. Do you, my gorgeous little man?'

Clementine tried to get a closer look. She'd never seen a sphynx before.

'I suppose I have to show myself inside then, do I, seeing that niece of mine has vanished,' Violet tutted.

'I can take you.' Clementine walked beside the woman. 'And I'm sorry about what I said, Aunt Violet. I didn't recognise you. You're much older than the lady on the wall near Grandpa.'

'Don't apologise,' said Violet tartly. 'In my experience most people don't usually mean it when they say sorry, and as you're just a child, I don't imagine that you ever mean it.'

Violet strode into the hall, leaving Clementine on the front steps wondering what she had meant. Clementine *was* sorry. She didn't know why Aunt Violet didn't believe her.

PIG
TALES

lementine Rose called Lavender to come inside. As soon as she heard her name the little pig ran towards her and the two of them headed off to find her mother.

'Hello Uncle Digby,' Clementine said, as she almost bumped into him. He just managed to steady the tea tray he was carrying.

'Ooh, ooh, careful, Clementine. Good afternoon, Lavender. Your mother tells me Aunt Violet has arrived a day early. I'm afraid it's not a surprise. She never was very reliable. Have you met her yet?' the old man asked.

'Yes, just a little while ago. I think I said the wrong thing,' Clementine said with a worried frown.

'My dear girl, no one ever says the right thing to that woman,' the butler said with a smile. 'But don't worry. We haven't seen her in years and I suspect that as soon as she's upset your mother to her satisfaction, she'll be off and we won't see her again for another ten years. I'd best get this tea to the guests in the front sitting room. Your mother is in the kitchen.'

'She's got a sphynx,' Clementine informed him.

Digby frowned. He looked at Clementine patiently and waited for her to explain further.

'It's in a bag and it hissed at me,' Clementine said. 'I hope it's not dangerous.'

Digby hoped so too.

Clementine skipped off to the kitchen with Lavender tripping along behind her. Lady

Clarissa was pulling teacups and their matching saucers down from the dresser.

'Hello Mummy,' the child said as she and Lavender entered the room. 'Where's Aunt Violet?'

'Upstairs.' Clarissa turned and Clementine noticed she was frowning. 'I had planned to put her in the Blue Room on the third floor but she insisted on having the Rose Room on the second with the bathroom attached. I'd kept that for the guests arriving this evening. I can't possibly charge the same rate for the other room. It's much smaller and not nearly as nice.' She bit her lip. 'And now the guests will have to share their bathroom, which they specifically asked not to.'

'Mummy, why don't you like Aunt Violet?' Clementine Rose asked as she pulled out a chair and sat at the kitchen table. Lavender lay down underneath and settled in for a snooze.

'It's a very long story but she was horrible to Grandpa and to me.'

'What about?' Clementine asked.

'Money,' her mother replied as she fetched the teapot from the stove.

'But we don't have any, so we don't have to worry about it,' Clementine said. She'd heard her mother say that to Uncle Digby lots of times.

Clarissa laughed. 'Yes, and I suppose that's the problem. Aunt Violet and your grandfather fought about money. You see, he inherited Penberthy House from his parents and Aunt Violet got a small allowance and nothing more.'

'But why didn't she get the house too?' Clementine asked.

'That's just how things worked then, I'm afraid. The eldest son got the house. But Grandpa and Aunt Violet had been very close when they were children and he always felt badly about it too, so over the years he gave Aunt Violet as much as he could. He even bought her a cottage so she'd have a home but Aunt Violet sold everything to pay for her expensive clothes and holidays.'

Clementine still looked confused.

'Your great-aunt likes the finer things in life,' her mother explained. 'But you don't need to worry about any of it, Clementine. I'm hoping that she'll be gone tomorrow.'

'I thought Grandpa looked a bit annoyed,' said Clementine, nodding.

'Did you think so, darling?' her mother asked fondly.

'Oh yes, he looked cross when I came inside,' the child said.

The walls in Penberthy House were lined with portraits of all the past owners and family members. A large painting of Clemmie's grandfather hung in the entrance hall, along with one of her grandmother and, she now knew, Aunt Violet. Clementine liked to talk to them from time to time, and was certain that they changed their expressions depending on what was going on around the house. She was sure that her grandmother laughed the first time Lavender tried to walk up the stairs and kept on slipping back down. Her grandfather had a kindly smile and Clementine often chatted to him about this and that. She liked to practise her poems for them as well. Lady Clarissa would often hear her daughter telling tales to the family. She thought it was wonderful that Clementine had such a vivid imagination.

The clacking of heels on the bare timber floor rang out a warning that someone was approaching.

'Is the tea ready yet?' Violet's voice entered the room before she did.

'Won't be a moment, Aunt Violet,' Clarissa said quickly and busied herself pouring boiling water into the teapot.

Clementine looked at her great-aunt. She wondered what had happened to the beautiful young woman in the portrait.

Violet stared back at Clementine.

'Am I to take tea in here? In the kitchen?' the old woman scoffed. 'While your friends are waited on hand and foot in the sitting room?'

Clarissa ignored Violet's questions and

placed a teacup and plate with a large slice of sponge cake on the table.

Violet stared at the tea and cake. 'Well, I suppose that's your answer.' She pulled out a chair and sat down. 'Is this Mother's good china?' The older woman lifted the plate and studied the underside.

'Yes, Aunt Violet,' Clarissa replied. 'I'm afraid I've had to use what we've got over the years. I can't afford to replace it.'

'This was only ever allowed out of the cupboard on Christmas Day. Mother would turn in her grave.' The woman shook her head. 'I should have taken it and sold it when I had the chance,' she whispered under her breath.

'Do you have milk, Aunt Violet?' Clarissa asked, hoping to steer her off the subject of the china.

'Of course I do. I should think you'd remember, Clarissa,' Violet snarled. She pointed at the cake. 'Did you make that?'

'No, I'm afraid not,' Clarissa said. 'I haven't had time today.'

'Pierre made it,' Clementine offered. 'He makes the best cakes ever.'

Violet tilted her chin upwards and gave Clementine a sidelong glance. 'We'll see about that.'

'Would you like to hear a poem?' Clementine asked.

'A what?' Violet sipped her tea.

'A poem,' Clementine replied. 'I know lots of them by heart and I have some funny ones too.'

'No, not particularly. In fact, I'd rather that you left the room,' Violet snapped. 'I need to speak to your mother. In private.'

'But Lavender's asleep,' said Clementine seriously.

'Who's Lavender? Don't tell me there's another child I don't know about?' Violet asked.

'Lavender's my pig,' Clementine said. 'She's a teacup.'

The woman's eyes widened and she stared at the teacup in her hand. 'You have a dirty, smelly pig? And it's called Lavender?'

'Pigs aren't dirty or smelly, Aunt Violet. Pigs

are smart and cuddly. Lavender's only as big as a cat, and she won't grow any more,' Clementine replied. 'That's why she's called a teacup pig.'

'What a load of nonsense,' Violet scoffed. 'I've never heard such tripe. Everyone knows that pigs are huge and disgusting and they live outside in sties. Off you go. Your mother and I need to talk. About you, among other things.'

'Aunt Violet, please don't speak to my daughter like that.' Clarissa spoke in a voice barely more than a whisper.

'But I can't go,' said Clementine with a scowl. 'I told you already. Lavender's asleep.' She was becoming more certain that her great-aunt was hard of hearing.

'Where is this so-called teacup pig?' asked Violet. 'I suppose you keep it in the kitchen, do you?'

'She's under my chair,' Clementine replied.

Aunt Violet gasped. She looked towards Clarissa, who nodded, then back at Clementine. The child pointed under her chair. Violet knelt down to look. Clementine Rose knelt down at

the other end of the table. Their eyes locked underneath.

'There she is,' Clementine whispered, and pointed. 'Please don't wake her up because she's very tired.' She put her finger to her lips.

Violet settled back into her chair.

'What sort of circus are you running here, Clarissa?' the old woman demanded. 'First a child, then a pig in the house and those friends of yours in the sitting room had the hide to ask me if I could get them some more soap for their bathroom – what do I look like? The hired help?' Violet placed her teacup on the table with a thud.

'I can explain,' Clarissa began.

Digby Pertwhistle entered the room, carrying the tea tray full of dirty cups and saucers. 'Good afternoon, Miss Appleby,' Digby said with a nod towards her. 'Welcome back to Penberthy House.'

'I can't believe that *you're* still here. I thought you'd have shuffled off years ago,' the woman snarled.

45

'And it's lovely to see you too.' Digby winked at Clementine as he went to the sink and began to unpack the tray.

'The place is falling down around your ears, Clarissa, and you still insist on having Pertwhistle here,' Violet hissed. 'I can't imagine how you pay the man.'

'Mummy wins things,' Clementine said.

Clarissa had hoped Clementine wouldn't bring that subject up.

'What do you mean?' Violet demanded.

'Mummy wins lots of competitions. She won that coffee machine and this whole kitchen and new beds for upstairs and even a holiday to Tahiti that Uncle Digby took last year,' Clementine explained. 'She won Lavender at the fair too, which was very lucky because teacup pigs cost a lot of money.'

'Well, aren't you just the fortunate one, Clarissa,' Violet said through pursed lips.

'How long are you staying, Aunt Violet?' Clementine asked.

'I haven't decided,' the woman replied.

Lady Clarissa and Digby Pertwhistle looked at each other, horrified at the thought of having to put up with the woman for any longer than a night.

'Mummy's very good at looking after people,' Clementine announced.

Clarissa and Digby gulped in unison. It was another of those times they both wished Clementine wasn't quite so honest.

'Clementine, why don't you take Lavender upstairs and put her in her basket?' her mother suggested. 'I'm sure you can do that without waking her up.'

Clementine peeked at the sleepy pig. Digby lifted the chair and Clementine picked her up, cradling her like a baby.

'That's the most ridiculous thing I've ever seen in my life,' Violet huffed, then shooed Clementine as if waving away a pesky fly. 'Well, hurry up then, off you go.'

When Aunt Violet wasn't looking, Clementine wrinkled her nose at the beastly woman.

THE
SPHYNX

Clementine Rose carried the dozing pig upstairs to her bedroom and laid her in her basket. Lavender stirred and grunted a couple of times but Clemmie tickled her tummy and soon she was fast asleep.

Clementine spent some time colouring in and practising the new poem Uncle Digby had taught her but after a while she felt fidgety.

She noticed that the house had fallen quiet. Usually that meant the guests were off on a ramble or having a rest in their rooms.

She kept thinking about Aunt Violet. The lady in the painting was much nicer to talk to than the woman downstairs. *She* was a bossy boots.

Then Clementine remembered the sphynx. Aunt Violet was staying downstairs on the second floor in the Rose Room. She left Lavender sound asleep and made her way along the hall and down the main staircase to the level below. The Rose Room was by far the biggest and prettiest in the whole house. It was also the one that her mother used to advertise the hotel. The room was at the end of the corridor and had a wonderful view of the garden on three sides. It was also the only room with a new bathroom, which had been installed after Lady Clarissa won a bathroom makeover package the year before.

Clementine knocked at the door. There was no answer so she turned the handle and opened it just enough to peek her head around.

'Hello, Aunt Violet, are you here?' she called. The room was silent.

Clementine looked about for the black bag. Uncle Digby must have brought up Aunt Violet's luggage from the car. Sitting on the floor at the end of the bed were three huge suitcases and a beauty case as well. Clementine thought that was a lot for someone staying just one night. Usually weekend guests had only half as much.

One of the suitcases was open. Clementine had a peek under the flap. Sitting on top of a pile of neatly folded clothes was a small gold clock and a bronze statue of a horse. There were some silver candlesticks too. She thought Aunt Violet must really like those things a lot to take them with her for a holiday.

A ruby velvet chaise longue sat underneath the side window. The fabric was a little frayed around the edges but Lady Clarissa had a clever way with throw rugs and cushions and could make the shabbiest of furniture seem well loved rather than in need of fixing. A tall cedar chest of drawers stood beside the doorway to the ensuite bathroom. A roll-top writing desk took up one corner of the room, and there was a dressing table too. On it sat a large vase full of red, pink and peach roses her mother had cut from the garden.

Clementine's favourite thing in the Rose Room was the enormous four-poster bed. It was so tall that you needed a special stepladder to climb onto it. When the house was empty, Clementine often spent time in this room, climbing up and down onto the bed. Lavender tried to get up too sometimes but her little legs just weren't long enough.

Clementine tiptoed around to the other side of the bed.

'Sphynx,' she whispered in a singsong voice, 'where are you?' Then she spotted the black bag sitting open on the floor. 'Oh!' Clementine gasped. The bag was empty. Maybe the creature was on the bed. She scooted up the little ladder onto the patchwork duvet and came face to face with the strangest creature she'd ever seen.

'Argh!' She drew in a sharp breath and kept

as still as she could. It was lying in the middle of the bed and had huge pointy ears and a strange wrinkly head. The beast half-opened its green eyes and glared at her.

Clementine had no idea what it was. It sort of looked like a giant rat or maybe a cat, but it didn't have any fur. The creature stared at her in a disgusted sort of way, just like the lady had looked at her when she had spilled the orange juice the week before.

Clementine gulped.

'What are you doing in here?' a voice demanded. Clementine Rose spun around to see Aunt Violet charging through the door. 'You leave my Pharaoh alone,' she growled.

'I . . . I didn't touch him, I promise,' Clementine protested.

'I told you before that he doesn't like children.' Violet strode towards the bed, her eyes scanning the room. 'Have you been snooping through my things?'

Clementine shook her head. 'No, of course not, Aunt Violet. Well, except that I saw your horse statue and some candlesticks and a clock. They must be very precious for you to bring them on holidays.'

'You little sneak.' Violet glimpsed the official-looking document poking out of the top of her handbag. The first words were: 'Eviction Notice'. She walked over and stuffed it back inside, wondering if Clementine could yet read.

Clementine gulped.

'Well, you shouldn't be in here,' Violet snapped.

'What . . . what is he?' Clementine asked.

'What's who?' Violet replied.

'Him.' Clementine pointed at the creature on the bed.

'He's a sphynx,' the old woman replied, rolling her eyes. 'I told you that earlier. Or are your ears full of wax?'

'No, Mummy cleans my ears every Thursday at bath time, except if I'm too tired and I don't have a bath, and then she does it on Friday,' Clementine said. 'I know he's a sphynx but what sort of creature is that?'

'It's a cat, of course, you silly child,' said Violet, shaking her head.

Clementine had never seen a cat like it before and she knew quite a few. There was Claws at the village shop and her friend Sophie had a fluffy white kitten called Mintie. Her other friend Poppy had lots of cats on the farm at Highton Hall and none of them looked even the slightest bit like Pharaoh.

'Is something wrong with him?' Clementine asked.

'Of course not.' Violet reached into the middle of the bed and patted the cat's wrinkly head.

'But . . .' Clementine wondered if she should tell Aunt Violet what she could see. Maybe the woman had something wrong with her eyesight as well as her hearing. Clementine decided that it was better to tell the truth. 'He's got no hair.'

'He was born that way,' Violet replied, as if it was the most usual thing in the world to have a bald cat. 'My *bootiful* boy.' Violet leaned across the bed and nuzzled against his face. The cat hissed at her.

Clementine wondered if Aunt Violet had taken him to the vet to see if there was a cure. Pharaoh was just about the ugliest creature she'd ever seen, apart from Father Bob's dribbly bulldog, Adrian.

'And what are you doing in my room, anyway?' Violet asked, glaring at Clementine.

The child gulped. She seemed to be asked that question quite a lot. 'I wanted to see what a sphynx was,' she replied.

'Well, now you have and I would thank you to stay out of *my* room, young lady.' Violet walked to the door and held it open.

Clementine slid down from the bed and walked towards her.

Violet stared at the child with her pretty blonde hair and ink-blue eyes. There was something vaguely familiar about her, yet the woman knew that was impossible. She'd never heard of her before today, let alone seen her.

'Off you go,' said Violet. 'I have things to do, and talking to you is not one of them.'

Clementine smiled at the old woman.

She had a habit of doing that when she was nervous.

'What are you grinning about?' Violet demanded.

'Nothing, Aunt Violet, nothing at all,' said Clementine, and scurried out the door.

A HAIRY STORY

After her visit with Pharaoh and Aunt Violet, Clementine Rose decided to find her mother and Uncle Digby and warn them about the bald sphynx. She wondered if they might have some ideas about a cure.

Clementine was on her way to the kitchen when she was distracted by a man. She heard him before she saw him – the loudest grunting snores ever. That was saying something because there had been plenty of snorers taking naps in the sitting room over the years. When she reached the bottom of the stairs she saw him in the winged armchair by the fireplace, with his head tilted back and his mouth wide open.

Clementine decided to take a closer look. She tiptoed into the room and stood beside the chair, resting her elbows on the arm with her head cradled in her hands. She thought he must be quite old. His forehead and cheeks were lined like crinkle-cut chips, and the skin on his neck hung loose, just like on the turkey Mr Mogg was keeping before last Christmas.

His hands were resting in his lap and she noticed they had lots of tan spots on them. Clementine liked watching the way the long hairs that stuck out of his nostrils fluttered in time with his breaths.

She glanced up at his hair. Most of the older men Clementine knew had grey or silver hair, like Mr Mogg and Father Bob, or not very much at all, like Uncle Digby. He just had a few long strands that he combed over the top and kept in place with some goo from a jar. This man's hair was dark orange and there was something not quite right about the way it was sitting. Clementine stood up on her tippy-toes and reached out to touch the thick crop. Her finger pressed against it gently. The man snorted loudly and she jumped back. Clemmie held her breath but his eyes stayed firmly shut. She wanted to touch his hair again – it felt rough, like the soap pad Uncle Digby used to scrub the saucepans. She reached up and stretched out her hand but just as she did, something terrible happened. As she made contact with the hair, it slid right off the top of his head and onto the floor.

Clemmie clutched her hands to her mouth. She'd never seen anyone's hair fall off like that before. The orange mop lay on the floor like a flat ginger cat. Clementine leaned down to get a closer look. She didn't want to touch it any more but somehow she had to get it back on top of the man's head.

Clementine gripped it between her pointer

finger and thumb and lifted it up slowly. Just as the hair was level with the top of the man's head, a fly began to buzz around his left ear. And right at the same time Clementine was about to deposit the hair back onto his head, the man stirred and swatted at the fly. He missed and flicked his hair right into the fireplace, where it erupted into flames and burnt away to nothing in seconds.

Clementine stood perfectly still and held her breath. She wondered if she could make him some new hair and tape it to his shiny head before he woke up. She remembered her old toy orangutan. Then she remembered that she'd lost it at her friend Poppy's house.

Maybe the man wouldn't notice. Maybe he had some more hair in his suitcase that he could wear instead. Maybe it would grow back before he woke up.

Clementine was staring at the man and wondering what to do, when out of the corner of her eye she saw a reflection of something moving in the mirror above the fireplace. It was just a flash but she knew that there was someone else in the room. The sitting room was shaped like a capital 'L', with another entrance from the back hallway. Clementine wondered if whoever it was had seen what happened with the man and his hair.

She decided to see who was there and tiptoed past the long floral sofa and the china cabinet to investigate. Clementine leaned around the corner in slow motion.

'Oh!' she gasped. Sticking up in the air was a bottom and it was attached to Aunt Violet. The old woman was down on her hands and knees with her head under the green velvet grandfather chair.

Clementine watched for a moment.

'Hello Aunt Violet,' she whispered.

There was a dull thud as Violet thwacked her head on the underside of the chair.

'Ow!' the woman grumbled as she wriggled out. 'You again!'

'Have you lost something?' Clementine asked.

'No, of course not.' Violet stood up and smoothed the front of her trousers. 'Have you?' She arched an eyebrow menacingly.

Clementine wondered if Aunt Violet had seen what happened to the man and his hair. She shook her head slowly.

She knew that she should tell the truth. It was just that, at the moment, she didn't quite know how. And after all, it was an accident.

Aunt Violet looked at Clementine and sniffed. Then she turned on her heel and strode out of the room.

Clementine tiptoed back towards the man without the hair. He was still fast asleep. She decided that the best plan was to find Uncle Digby and tell him the truth. He would know what to do.

TRUTH
TIME

Clementine Rose found Digby Pertwhistle in the dining room, setting
the huge mahogany table for dinner.

'Hello Clemmie,' he said. 'What have you
been up to now?'

Clementine gulped. She wondered if Uncle
Digby had special powers. He always seemed
to know when there was trouble about.

'Nothing much,' she replied, not quite ready
to talk about the burnt hair. 'I met Aunt Violet's
sphynx.'

'Oh, yes, and what sort of a creature is this sphynx?' Digby asked.

'Aunt Violet says that he's a cat but he's the strangest looking cat I've ever seen. He's got no hair,' Clementine explained. 'But I don't think she can see that.'

Digby considered this. 'Interesting.'

'He's not interesting,' Clementine replied. 'He's ugly.'

'Perhaps he has a special personality,' said Digby.

Clementine shook her head. 'I don't think so. He even hissed at Aunt Violet.'

'Sounds like a smart cat if you ask me,' said Digby, his lips twitching. He continued putting the cutlery in place.

'Uncle Digby, I need to tell you something,' said Clementine. She took a small step closer to the man, then another, until she stood right beside him.

He turned and bent down to meet her gaze. 'Uh-oh. What have you done now, Clementine?'

'Well,' she began, 'I didn't mean to but it just sort of happened.'

'I have to get some wine from the cellar,' said Digby. 'Why don't you come with me and you can explain on the way.'

Clementine nodded.

On the evenings they had guests, Clementine, her mother and Digby Pertwhistle usually ate in the kitchen before the meal was served. But tonight Clarissa wasn't quite sure what to do. Aunt Violet wasn't a paying guest but she was expecting to be served in the dining room.

After his visit to the cellar with Clementine, Digby Pertwhistle was as puzzled by what to do about the man and his missing hair as Clementine was.

She hadn't realised exactly how tricky a subject hair was. When her mother told her that they would be eating in the dining room with Aunt Violet and the guests, Clementine

asked if she could have dinner with Uncle Digby instead.

'No, Clemmie,' her mother replied. 'I need you to be charming to everyone and hopefully Aunt Violet will behave herself. Digby, I hope you don't mind serving all of us tonight.'

'Of course not, my dear. Although perhaps if you made Violet eat her dinner out here in the kitchen with us as we usually do, she might pack her bags and head for home,' Digby suggested.

'I had thought of that,' said Clarissa, 'but I don't want her making a fuss and upsetting the guests, which she's sure to do if we leave her out here. She still doesn't know that we run the house as a hotel. She's such a terrible snob. I can't imagine she'll be pleased when she finds out. Mrs Mogg is coming to help with dinner so I can look after Aunt Violet. And I *still* don't know why she's here. She won't give me a straight answer.'

'Maybe she wants to make up and be friends,' Clementine suggested. 'And give you a present. She has lots of things in her suitcase.'

'*How* do you know what she has in her suitcase?' asked Clarissa, casting her daughter a stern look. 'I hope you haven't been snooping, young lady.'

Clementine shook her head. 'I went to visit her and her bag was open and she has candlesticks and a clock and even a bronze statue of a horse.'

'Really? Why would she bring all of that with her?' Clarissa bit her lip and looked thoughtful, then shook herself and said, 'Anyway, Clementine, run along and put on a fresh dress and then come straight back down to the dining room. And no more spying.'

Clementine nodded. 'I'm going to wear my green stripes with the pink cardigan. Can Lavender come too?'

'Oh no, Clemmie, not tonight. Make sure that she has a fresh bowl of water and her litter box is clean and I'll take her up some pellets,' her mother instructed. 'I don't think Lavender would improve Aunt Violet's mood at all.'

The child skipped off up the back stairs that led from the kitchen to the upper levels. She opened her bedroom door and found Lavender pushing a little ball all over the floor. The pig squealed when she saw her mistress.

'Hello Lavender.' Clementine gave the tiny pig a scratch on the top of her head. 'Sorry, but Mummy says you have to stay up here tonight. We've got to eat dinner with the guests in the dining room and I'm scared about seeing the man from the sitting room,' she explained to the pig, who had scrambled into her lap and was enjoying a rub on her grey belly. 'I think Aunt Violet's going to tell on me.'

Lavender grunted and closed her eyes.

'I told Uncle Digby what happened and he said that perhaps we should just wait and see. But I don't know what we're waiting for and I already know what we'll see. That man is as bald as Aunt Violet's cat. I haven't told you about him, have I? He's very strange,' said Clementine, looking at Lavender's pink tummy. 'I suppose you don't really have much hair either,' she observed, 'but you're a pig and you're not meant to have hair. Cats are.'

Clementine placed Lavender back on the floor and checked the water bowl and litter box, which was over in the corner of the room behind a screen. Then she took her green striped dress from the wardrobe and changed.

'Be good, Lavender, and I'll bring you some vegetables.' Clementine pulled on her cardigan and sat down to buckle her pink shoes.

Lavender grunted and waddled over to her basket.

'I'll see you after dinner.' Clementine quickly ran a brush through her hair and found a green hairclip to pin back the sweep of blonde hair that covered her eyes. 'There.'

A NIGHT TO
REMEMBER

The guests were gathered in the dining room by the time Clementine arrived. Her mother was chatting away while Uncle Digby offered champagne. Aunt Violet hadn't yet appeared.

'Clementine, come and meet everyone,' her mother instructed. There were two couples and a single lady staying in the house. 'This is Mr and Mrs O'Connell.' Clarissa nodded at a man wearing a smart sports coat and his wife, who wore a lovely tangerine-coloured silk shirt with white pants. 'This is my daughter, Clementine Rose,' Clarissa told them.

'Hello there, Clementine Rose,' the man said. 'Aren't you a lucky girl to live in a lovely big house like this?'

'Hello,' Clementine smiled. 'Yes, but I wish it didn't have so many holes in the roof.'

Mr and Mrs O'Connell exchanged quizzical looks.

'Come along, darling, and meet our other guests.' Clarissa guided Clementine away. She introduced her to a younger woman with long dark hair. 'This is Miss Herring. She's writing a book, Clementine, isn't that exciting?'

'Hello,' Clementine said. 'Does it have lots of pictures? I can't read yet but I'm going to big school soon and then I'll be able to.'

'No, I'm afraid that it doesn't have any pictures at all,' Miss Herring replied. 'It's about business.'

Clementine wrinkled her nose. 'It sounds a bit . . . boring,' she whispered.

'Clementine, I'm sure Miss Herring's book is wonderful,' her mother rebuked.

Miss Herring smiled thinly.

'Now, Clementine, I want you to meet Mr and Mrs Sparks.' Clarissa took Clemmie's hand and led her to the other side of the room.

Clementine gulped. The man and woman appeared to be having an argument, except that it was all whispers and his face looked red and cross.

'Oh, for heaven's sake, Floyd, I've told you a thousand times that no one stole your wretched hairpiece and if they did, I'd have to find them and thank them for getting rid of the ridiculous thing anyway,' the woman said, rolling her eyes.

'Is everything all right?' Clarissa asked.

'Yes, my dear. Floyd's lost his toupee and he thinks someone must have stolen it while he was having a nap this afternoon. I can't imagine for one second who would want to steal it – it was quite revolting and I've been telling him for years that he looks much better without it,' Mrs Sparks explained.

Clementine stood beside her mother, wondering if she should say anything.

'And who do we have here?' asked Mrs Sparks, as she looked at Clementine.

'This is my daughter, Clementine Rose,' Clarissa said.

'Hello dear, it's a pleasure to meet you and I must say I love your dress,' said Mrs Sparks. She smiled at Clemmie, then dug her elbow into her husband's ribs.

'Oh hello,' the man said. 'You look like a smart girl. You didn't happen to see my hair anywhere this afternoon, did you?'

Clementine was just about to tell him what happened when Mrs Sparks interrupted them.

'Oh, Floyd Sparks, stop talking about that ridiculous rug. Clementine, dear, I hope the jolly thing ended up in the fire. He looks so much more handsome without it. It was orange, too. Can you believe a man of his age, wearing something so ridiculous? He hasn't had orange hair in years anyway. Jolly thing looked like a dead ginger cat on top of his head. Now tell me, Clementine, how old are you?'

'I'm five,' the child replied, trying not to smile. She was imagining a ginger cat sitting on top of Mr Sparks's head.

'How wonderful to be five,' Mrs Sparks enthused. 'You must tell me, what do five-year-olds like to get up to these days? I bet you must have lots of fun roaming about this big house of yours.'

'My friends are coming tomorrow to stay for the night,' Clementine said. 'And I'm going to ask Mummy if we can have a camp-out.'

'Oh my dear, that sounds wonderful,' Mrs Sparks nodded.

Lady Clarissa didn't comment. She was watching the door. 'Excuse me, Mr and Mrs Sparks, I see Aunt Violet has arrived,' she said. She made her way to the door where Violet was surveying the scene.

'You *do* have a rather strange group of friends, Clarissa,' the woman hissed.

'Come along, Aunt Violet, I've put you at the end of the table near Clementine and me.' Clarissa guided the woman into the room.

'I like your dress, Aunt Violet,' Clementine told the old woman. The print had circles in all different shades of green. Clementine liked the way it swirled around.

'Yes, it's lovely, isn't it?' said Violet. She looked at the child and couldn't help thinking her own selection of clothing was rather sweet too – although she wasn't about to tell her.

Digby Pertwhistle re-entered the room and asked that the guests be seated. He then walked around the table placing the napkins into each of the diner's laps.

'Aunt Violet, I'd like to introduce you to Edward and Sandra O'Connell,' said Clarissa, nodding towards the couple sitting opposite her aunt.

'Charmed, I'm sure,' Violet sneered.

'Hello,' the couple replied in unison.

'And this is Becca Herring,' Clarissa introduced the young woman, then turned to the couple at the end of the table. 'And Zelda and Floyd Sparks. This is my aunt, Violet Appleby.'

Violet frowned but said, 'Hello.' She looked the couple up and down. 'I saw you earlier this afternoon, Mr Sparks, but there's something different about you now.'

'He's lost his hair,' Zelda Sparks offered. 'And he looks all the better for it.'

'I see. And where did you lose your hair exactly?' Violet asked.

'Well, I was having a nap in the sitting room and then when I woke up it was gone,' Floyd explained.

Violet turned and stared at Clementine. 'Really? A nap in the sitting room, this afternoon?'

Clementine gulped.

'Never mind, Mr Sparks,' Violet said. 'I've always thought a man looks much better if he just lets nature take its course. And there is nothing quite as ridiculous as a man of a certain age trying to be something he's not.'

Floyd nodded sheepishly.

'Yes, Miss Appleby, I couldn't agree more,' Zelda Sparks replied. 'Now, tell me, do you live in this magnificent residence too?'

'No, Aunt Violet's just visiting,' Clementine said, smiling at her great-aunt.

'Oh look, here's the entree,' Lady Clarissa said hastily. She was wishing she'd served Aunt Violet dinner in the kitchen with the family. 'Tonight we have mushroom soup with sourdough bread.'

There was a murmur of approval around the table. Violet placed her spoon into the thick brown liquid and drew it to her lips. She was pleasantly surprised by the taste.

'How's Pharaoh?' Clementine asked her great-aunt.

The old woman looked down her nose at Clemmie. 'What?'

'Your cat? Is he feeling well?' Clementine said.

'How would I know?' Violet retorted. 'He can't speak, you know.'

'Lavender can't speak either but I always

know how she's feeling. When she's happy she runs around a lot and when she's sad she sits in her basket and rests her head on the side and she won't come when I call her. But that's only happened a couple of times. Once when Mrs Mogg's cat Claws scratched her on the nose, and one day when I had to leave her at home to have my "look-see" day at school,' Clementine explained.

Violet rolled her eyes at the child and turned to speak with Becca Herring.

Clementine stared at Aunt Violet's back and wrinkled her nose.

Digby cleared away the soup bowls and returned with the main course. He set the steaming plates down in front of each guest.

'Ooh, this looks lovely, Lady Clarissa,' exclaimed Floyd Sparks. His mood seemed to have improved vastly.

Clarissa smiled at her guest.

Clementine pushed her fork into the baked potato on her plate and swirled it in the thick gravy.

'Clemmie, remember your manners, please,' her mother tutted.

Clementine frowned. She hadn't forgotten her manners. She just wanted some gravy on her potato.

As the meal progressed, Violet couldn't help but wonder about her niece's friends. They didn't seem to know Clarissa very well at all.

'What a wonderful roast,' said Mr O'Connell as he finished the last bite of his lamb and placed his knife and fork together on the plate. 'We'll definitely be telling our friends about Penberthy House.'

Clarissa smiled thinly. 'Thank you, Mr O'Connell.'

'Why would you be telling your friends?' Violet asked.

'Well, your niece is quite the loveliest hostess and the wife and I haven't stayed in as nice a place as this for a long time. Although that bathroom upstairs could do with a bit of updating and I have noticed the wallpaper's falling down in a couple of spots.'

Violet glanced around the table. All of a sudden she realised exactly what was going on.

'Clarissa, I'd like a word. In private,' she said through clenched teeth.

Clarissa did her best to put the woman off. 'But Aunt Violet, we're about to have dessert.'

'And it's going to be yum, yum, yummy,' Clementine sang. 'Mrs Mogg made chocolate mousse and I love chocolate mousse.'

The rest of the group laughed.

'We won't be long.' Violet stood up and waited for Clarissa to do the same. The younger woman led the older one out of the dining room, along the hallway and into the library.

The library at Penberthy House held a magnificent collection of over ten thousand dusty, leather-bound books, some dating back hundreds of years. There was a fireplace and shelves from the floor to the ceiling, with a spiral staircase leading up to a balcony that ran around the top half of the room. A magnificent mahogany desk sat in the centre of the floor and there were old floral couches to sit on too, although most of them needed new springs and the covers were getting tatty.

Clarissa hoped that was far enough away that the guests wouldn't hear their conversation.

Violet closed the door and turned to her niece, blocking the way out. 'Clarissa, those people in there are not your friends.'

'No, Aunt Violet, they're not,' Clarissa replied.

'Well, what are they doing here?' the old woman demanded.

'They're staying for the weekend,' said Clarissa. She took a deep breath. 'So that I can keep Penberthy House.'

'So, all of those people are paying you to stay here?' Violet snapped.

'Yes, Aunt Violet. I've been running the house as a country hotel for years,' Clarissa replied. 'The repairs won't pay for themselves.'

'What happened to all that money your father left you?' Violet asked. 'He'd turn in his grave knowing you were renting the place to strangers.'

'There was only ever a little money, Aunt Violet, despite what you always thought. Father was a generous man and he had given away most of the family fortune. In fact, he gave a good deal of it to you. I'm sure that he never realised just how much it costs to look after this place,' Clarissa explained.

'You're telling me that Penberthy House is falling down because you can't afford to do any better?' Violet asked.

'Yes, there's no pot of gold,' Clarissa said firmly. 'And if you don't like what I'm doing then you can leave.'

'How dare you? I'm family. And I'll go when, and if, I'm ready,' Violet huffed. Her eyes darted around the room. 'What have you changed in here?' she demanded, still scanning the length and breadth of the library.

'Digby removed that horrid old cabinet that used to sit in front of the shelves at the end of the row, that's all.'

Violet walked towards the bookshelf. She drew in a sharp breath as if a memory had just

85

surfaced. 'Did he find anything behind it?' she asked.

'What do you mean?'

'Anything unusual?' Violet prompted.

Clarissa wondered what she was talking about. 'Just books and shelves. It always looked odd jutting out at the end and covering the row. It looks much better now, don't you think?'

'Yes, much better.' Violet smirked, then spun around and stalked off down the hallway towards the grand staircase.

Clarissa shook her head. Surely Aunt Violet wasn't planning to stay forever.

Meanwhile, back in the dining room, Digby Pertwhistle was serving dessert and Clementine Rose was entertaining the guests with one of her favourite poems. It was by a very famous man called Roald Dahl and it was about a crocodile.

She was imagining the crocodile had a face just like Aunt Violet's, but only half as mean.

The guests clapped loudly as she finished with a bow.

SLEEPOVER

By midday on Sunday the guests had all departed, except Aunt Violet, who had vanished after breakfast, leaving a trail of belongings strewn around the Rose Room.

Clementine was helping her mother take the sheets off the guest beds and wondering how long it would be until Sophie and Jules arrived. 'Where's Uncle Digby?' she asked.

'He's in the library. He said he wanted to give the place a spring clean,' Clarissa explained.

'Uncle Digby works hard, doesn't he, Mummy?' said Clementine.

88

'Yes, he does. We're lucky to have him,' her mother said with a nod.

'I've been thinking,' Clementine began.

'Uh-oh,' Clarissa smiled.

'It's nothing bad, Mummy. I was just wondering if we can have a camp-out tonight.'

Her mother frowned. 'But where do you want to camp this time?' When Clementine, Sophie and Jules last had a 'camp-out', it was in the front sitting room under a giant tent made from bedsheets, on a floor of cushions.

Clementine thought for a moment. They all liked camping in the Rose Room, where they could turn the four-poster bed into a giant tent. But that was off limits because Aunt Violet was there.

'Can we camp in the attic?' Clementine asked.

'No, Clemmie, it's jam-packed with all sorts of things and I think you might find it a little on the creepy side,' her mother replied. Clarissa didn't like going up there in the middle of the day, let alone the thought of staying there all night.

'What about the library?' Clementine suggested.

'Perfect,' her mother said. 'And at least there won't be any dust, either.'

Clementine loved the library. It was one of her favourite rooms in the whole house.

'Why don't you go and get some pillows from the linen press and take them downstairs,' her mother suggested. 'I can finish up here.'

Clementine nodded. 'Come on, Lavender,' she called to the tiny pig, who was snuffling about under the bed. 'We've got to get your basket and blanket and all the duvets and at least one hundred pillows.'

Clarissa smiled to herself. She couldn't imagine how dull her life would have been without Clementine.

Clementine dragged piles of pillows and duvets downstairs to the library where Digby Pertwhistle was almost finished cleaning.

After their second run, Lavender stayed behind and settled in for a nap under one of the armchairs.

As Clementine charged up the back stairs to her bedroom, she caught sight of Aunt Violet coming out of the room. She was tucking something sparkly into the pocket of her trousers.

'Hello Aunt Violet,' Clementine called. 'Were you looking for me?'

The old woman shot into the air and spun around.

'Good heavens, child, do you make a habit of sneaking up on people or do you reserve that especially for me?' she snarled.

'I didn't mean to.'

'Well, you did. And no, I wasn't looking *for you*,' Violet said with a small snort of disbelief.

'But you were in my room,' Clementine said, remembering how cross Aunt Violet had been when she had visited the Rose Room.

'It was *my* room, actually, when I was a girl. And I was just looking,' Violet replied.

'Did you like it?' Clementine asked.

'No, it was much prettier when it was mine. But I suppose we could always fix it up to the way it should be. Perhaps I'd like to have it again.'

'But it's *my* room now,' Clementine said.

'You could move,' said Violet. 'This is a big house.'

Clementine wondered what her great-aunt was talking about. She wasn't moving out of her room.

'Are you staying for a long time, Aunt Violet?' Clementine asked.

'That depends. Has Pertwhistle finished in the library yet?' the old woman demanded.

'No. Uncle Digby's doing a spring clean and they take ages and then my friends are coming to stay for the night and we're having a camp-out,' Clementine explained.

'What friends?' asked Violet.

'Sophie and Jules. They live in Highton Mill. Their father Pierre makes all of those lovely cakes you like to eat,' Clementine prattled.

'Village children?' Violet frowned. 'Don't you have any more suitable friends?'

Clementine was puzzled. 'I don't know what you mean, Aunt Violet.'

'I'm exhausted,' the woman declared. 'Tell your mother to bring me a cup of tea in my room. I've got a headache coming on.'

Clementine watched as her great-aunt strode along the hallway to the main staircase. Surely she couldn't take her room away. Grandpa would have something to say about that.

SOPHIE
AND JULES

'Now, make sure that you do everything Clarissa asks and don't get into any trouble,' Odette instructed her two children as they stood on the driveway beside Clementine and her mother.

'Come on, Odette, we 'ave to get all the way to Downsfordvale before dark,' Pierre called from the driver's seat.

Odette gave her children a kiss on each cheek and then did the same to Clementine and Clarissa.

'*Sacrebleu*, Odette, 'urry up. It's only for one night. We will come back and get them tomorrow. Maybe.' Pierre grinned and shrugged his shoulders.

'That's fine with us, Papa,' Jules told his father. 'We love it here.'

'Maybe your Mama and me, we'll leave you with Lady Clarissa for a week and take an 'oliday,' Pierre teased.

'We're having a camp-out,' said Clementine. 'That's like a holiday.'

'In the library,' Sophie added, as her mother closed the passenger door.

'*Au revoir*,' Odette called.

'Goodbye,' the children chorused as the little van sped off down the driveway.

Lady Clarissa would gladly have kept Sophie and Jules for a week. Jules was a wonderful big brother to Sophie, and he and Clementine got along famously too.

'Come on then, what would you all like for afternoon tea?' Clarissa asked. 'Your father has left me half the patisserie, I think.'

'Chocolate brownie for me,' Sophie said.

'Chocolate eclair for me,' Jules said.

'Is there a meringue?' Clementine was imagining the sweet tingly confection melt away in her mouth.

'Several, I think,' Clarissa nodded.

'Yum! We need to have lots of energy if we're going camping in the library,' said Clementine.

'Why?' Sophie asked, her brown eyes wide.

'Because we're going on a safari,' said Clementine, as if it was obvious. 'Just like Grandpa did when he was young, except we're not going to shoot the animals, we'll just take some photographs.'

Jules laughed. 'So this is another adventure of yours, Clementine. Like last time when you said that all the people in the portraits on the walls had come to life and you told us about them.' Sophie and Jules loved Clementine's stories.

Clementine nodded. The three children followed Lady Clarissa into the entrance hall and Lavender trotted along behind.

'Do you remember when I told you about that lady up there?' Clementine pointed at Aunt Violet's portrait. 'I said that her name was Grace and she was beautiful and kind.'

Sophie and Jules nodded.

'Well, that's not her name.'

Lady Clarissa disappeared into the hallway on her way to the kitchen.

'What is her name?' Sophie asked.

'It's Violet and she's not beautiful. She's snappy and cross, and she's asleep upstairs,' Clementine said.

Sophie and Jules gasped.

'But I thought she was dead, like your grandfather,' Sophie said, her mouth gaping.

'I thought so too, but she came on Friday,' Clementine explained. 'And I don't think she likes me very much and she definitely doesn't like Lavender. She has a sphynx that looks like a giant rat and this afternoon she said that she might like to have my bedroom. But she does wear nice clothes and she has some of the loveliest shoes I've ever seen and she didn't tell on me last night about Mr Sparks's hair.'

'What happened to Mr Sparks's hair?' Sophie asked.

'It's complicated,' Clementine replied. 'I'll tell you later.'

'Maybe she just doesn't know you very well yet,' Jules suggested.

'Maybe, but she really doesn't like Uncle Digby,' Clementine confirmed.

'We should stay out of her way, then,' Jules decided. 'Your house is so big we shouldn't have to see her at all.'

The two girls nodded.

'Come on, let's get something to eat and then we can start building our tents.' Clementine raced off towards the kitchen with Sophie, Jules and Lavender hot on her heels.

CAMPING
OUT

The children had a wonderful afternoon setting up camp in the library. Lavender played hide and seek, running in and out from under the bedsheets that the girls were using to make their tents. Clementine convinced Uncle Digby to light a fire in the library hearth. She told him that a camp wasn't 'proper' unless there was a camp fire and, besides, a chill breath of wind was swirling through the house, a sign of a storm to come. Late in the afternoon, Mrs Mogg appeared

with a delivery of groceries for Lady Clarissa including a giant packet of marshmallows and some extra-long skewers.

By half past five, when Lady Clarissa brought their tea, Clementine, Sophie and Jules had transformed a corner of the enormous library using sheets, pegs and various bits of furniture. Clementine and Sophie had set up their beds under the desk, with a sheet over the top. Jules had a much more elaborate tent. It hung from the gallery upstairs and draped over a padded bench seat, giving him enough space inside to lie down or stand up.

'Well hello, my adventurers,' Lady Clarissa called as she carried in a tray with three plates of creamy scrambled eggs on hot buttered toast. Digby Pertwhistle followed close behind with three steaming mugs of hot chocolate and a bowl of vegetables for Lavender.

'Hello Mummy, hello Uncle Digby.' Clementine poked her head out from under the desk and greeted the pair. 'Do you like our camp site? We're on safari in Africa.'

'Yes, darling, it's wonderful,' Lady Clarissa said, smiling as she surveyed Clementine's stuffed toys, which the children had positioned around the room. 'Look at all those animals! And I love the way you've made your tent two-storeys, Jules. That's terribly clever.'

'I love camping at your house,' Jules replied. 'It's much better than when Papa took us to Gertrude's Grove for a weekend and it rained and rained and our tent had a hole in the roof. At least in here, we won't get wet.'

'Don't bet on it, young man.' Digby Pertwhistle set his tray on a small table beside the desk. 'I heard the forecast was for storms tonight and I was about to get some buckets. Depending on how bad it gets, you might have a drip or two right above your head.'

'Just a couple of drips are okay. On our camping trip we were soaked and Mama said that it was the most terrible weekend of her life,' said Jules as he straightened the sheet.

'All right, big game hunters, come and have your supper while it's hot,' Clarissa called.

'We're not hunters, Mummy,' Clementine said. 'We're wildlife photographers. See?' She reached under the desk and passed her mother an old Polaroid camera.

'Heavens, where did you find that?' Clarissa took it from her daughter and examined the contraption, before giving it back.

'Uncle Digby found it and it still works,' said Clementine. She pointed the camera at her mother, snapped the shutter and a photograph whirred out of the front of the machine.

'Gosh, I think I won that when I was a teenager. I haven't seen it for years but at the time I thought it was the fanciest thing going.' Clarissa laughed at the memory. 'Well, I hope you find some elephants and tigers and maybe even a lion or two in here tonight. But save your shots for the most exciting things because I think the film runs out quite quickly.'

Jules clasped the front of his tent together with two clothes pegs and joined the girls near the fire.

'Would you like Uncle Digby to come back

and tell you a story later?' said Clarissa with a wink at the old man. 'When I was a little girl he used to tell me wonderful tales about African safaris.'

Digby Pertwhistle shook his head. 'Oh, my dear, I think I've almost forgotten about my African adventures.'

'No!' Clementine Rose complained. 'Please tell us a story, Uncle Digby.'

'Yes, please, Uncle Digby,' Sophie added.

Lavender looked up and grunted.

'See, everyone wants you to,' Jules insisted.

'Well, eat your supper and I'll be back with the marshmallows in a little while,' Digby agreed.

Clarissa and Digby retreated to the kitchen and left the children to eat their fireside feast.

A branch outside banged against the window as the wind picked up speed.

'I hate storms,' said Sophie.

'I love them,' Clementine said, as she loaded her fork with a mouthful of scrambled eggs.

'You have to be brave, Sophie,' her brother

told her. 'Like Clementine. The storm can't hurt you.'

'But I don't like the lightning and the thunder,' his sister said. 'It sounds like a giant in a bad temper.'

'I think it's a giant having a party,' Clementine replied. 'Anyway, tonight we're together so nothing can hurt us.'

Jules raised his mug of hot chocolate in the air. 'Let's have a toast to our camping safari.'

Clementine raised her mug and nudged Sophie to do the same.

'To our camping safari,' the girls chorusèd. Lavender snorted happily.

GHOST SAFARI

At half past eight, after a wonderful tale about mischief-making monkeys and a hippo who liked to eat liquorice, the children brushed their teeth and crawled into their makeshift beds. Outside, the rain had begun to splatter against the windows but within minutes the only noise inside the tents was the shallow breathing of little bodies and a small squeak coming from Lavender, who was also fast asleep.

Clarissa peeked in on the group, switched

off the children's torches and closed the library door.

Aunt Violet had stayed in her room for the rest of the day. Clarissa had taken her a tea tray of boiled eggs and toasty soldiers for her supper, but Violet was fast asleep. Beside her, Pharaoh opened one eye and stared at his hostess, then curled his lip. Clarissa thought Clementine was quite right when she said that he was the strangest creature she'd ever seen.

Clarissa looked at the bags and clothes covering the room. Her aunt certainly had a lot of luggage with her. She walked over to straighten the cushions on the chaise longue and noticed a letter on the desk.

Clarissa leaned in to take a closer look, scanning the page. She glanced towards the bed where her aunt slept. 'So that's why you're here,' she whispered. She couldn't imagine what it would be like to have nowhere to go. And while Aunt Violet was a lot of things, cranky and rude being top of the list, she was also family.

Just after 10 pm, Digby Pertwhistle retired to his room. It wasn't long afterwards that Lady Clarissa made a final check on the children and went up to bed too.

Outside, the wind was beginning to howl. A loose shutter on the far end of the house had started to bang and Clarissa hoped that it didn't wake anyone. She hated the thought of having to go and attend to it in her nightdress, but it wouldn't be the first time. Overhead, thunder rumbled but down in the library the children slept without stirring.

Clementine was in the middle of a lovely dream about her grandpa. She was telling him a new poem she had learned when suddenly lightning tore open the darkness and filled the library with light. She awoke with a start and felt as if she was falling through a giant hole in the sky.

It took her a few moments to remember where she was.

Clementine lay awake under the desk as the light flickered around her. Goosebumps suddenly sprang up along her arms. It wasn't just the storm – she had a feeling there was someone else in the room. She crept to the edge of the tent and pulled open the sheets. A figure dressed in white stood at the end of the room. It had silver hair and bare feet and there was a glow coming from the end of its arm. Clementine wondered if it was one of her ancestors, perhaps from the portraits on the walls. She watched as the ghost pulled some books from the shelf. Clementine rubbed her eyes and wondered if she was still dreaming.

'I knew it,' a voice whispered. 'I knew you were in here. And now you're mine.'

It was the ghost speaking. Clementine reached for the camera beside her.

Sophie stirred. 'What are you doing?' she yawned.

'Shhhh!' Clementine pressed her finger against Sophie's lips. 'There's a ghost out there.'

Sophie's eyes widened. 'A ghost? On our safari?'

'I'm going to take its picture,' Clementine whispered.

Sophie shook her head. 'No!'

'Stay here.' Clementine began to crawl out from under the desk.

The ghost had its back to her. It turned around and at the same time a huge streak of lightning lit up the window and the whole library.

'Oh!' The ghost caught its breath. 'Who's there?' it whispered urgently when it saw Jules's two-storey tent.

Clementine crept in front of the white figure and pressed the button on the camera. The flash went off and Aunt Violet stood frozen to the spot.

'You again! What are you doing?' she demanded.

'Phew!' Clementine let out the breath she had been holding. 'I thought you were a ghost, Aunt Violet!'

Sophie scrambled out from under the desk. 'What's that?' she asked, pointing at Aunt Violet's hand.

Jules was awake now too. He wriggled out of his tent to join the girls. The children had Violet surrounded.

'Go back to sleep,' she ordered. 'You're all dreaming. I am a ghost. You are asleep and I was never here. Now give me that.' She reached out and tried to snatch the photograph that had whirred out of the old camera.

'What's going on in here?' Lady Clarissa flicked on the library lights. 'Aunt Violet! What on earth?'

Digby Pertwhistle hadn't been able to sleep either and was on his way to the kitchen to make a cup of cocoa when he heard the kerfuffle.

'Is that you, Violet?' he asked, squinting at the old woman in her nightgown.

Violet tried to hide whatever it was she was holding behind her back.

But Clementine handed her mother the picture that was coming to life in front of them.

'Is that . . .' Clarissa hesitated, peering at the image. 'Is that the Appleby tiara?' She handed the photograph to Digby Pertwhistle.

'Oh, my dear, I think it is. That tiara and the matching necklace and earrings have been missing for years. Your mother always thought the set had been stolen. You know it's worth a fortune.'

'Is that the tiara Granny's wearing in the portrait?' Clementine asked her mother. 'The one with all the sparkles?' She turned to her great-aunt. 'This morning when you were coming out of my room, Aunt Violet, I saw something twinkly in your hand and then you put it in your pocket. What was that?'

'It was none of your business,' the old woman replied.

'Aunt Violet, please don't speak to Clementine like that. What else did you find?'

'Mummy's earrings,' Violet said, pouting.

'We'll deal with those later. May I have the tiara, please?' Clarissa asked.

'No! It's mine!' the woman snapped.

Digby frowned at her and shook his head softly. 'I think you'll find it belongs to Clarissa.'

'Everything belongs to Clarissa,' Violet yelled. 'The house, the furniture, the china. But this is mine. And so are the earrings and the necklace. I found them when I was little and I hid them in different places in the house. I forgot about them until I was packing up the flat and found an old photograph of Mother wearing them. I couldn't think where the tiara was and then yesterday when I saw that the cabinet was gone, I remembered. You're not having it. I, I, I need it.' Violet's lip trembled and it looked as if she was going to cry.

'Aunt Violet, why don't you give it to me and I'll put it somewhere safe and we can talk about it in the morning,' Clarissa said soothingly.

'No!' The woman shuddered. 'You don't know what it's like. I haven't got any money left. None at all.' Violet began to wail. 'I don't even have anywhere to live!'

'I know,' Clarissa said, as she and Digby exchanged glances.

'It's all right, Aunt Violet,' said Clementine. 'We don't have any money either. And we have plenty of space. You could stay here with us if you like. But you can't have my bedroom,' she added. 'Grandpa said so. And you should try to be a bit kinder, like Mummy said you used to be.'

Violet was cornered. She jammed the tiara on top of Clementine's head and stomped past Clarissa.

'But I'm keeping the earrings, and the necklace too if I can remember where it is,' she said as she turned and stared at the group. Then she fled upstairs to her room.

'Why is Aunt Violet so mad?' Clementine asked her mother.

'I think she's embarrassed,' said Clarissa thoughtfully. 'She's been very sneaky.'

Clementine lifted the tiara from her head and stared at the sparkling jewels. 'It's lovely, Mummy.'

'Yes it is, Clemmie,' her mother replied. 'And I'm going to put it away in a very safe place.'

She strode to the opposite end of the bookshelf, reached up, and rested her hand on the spine of one of the books. The shelf spun around, revealing a safe buried in the wall.

'I think that's a very good idea,' said Digby.

'It's okay, Lady Clarissa, we're on safari,' Jules declared. 'Nothing can get past the wildlife photographers.'

Lady Clarissa spun the dial and swivelled the books back into place. 'All right, off to sleep everyone,' she instructed, 'or you'll never get up in the morning.'

Clementine kissed her mother goodnight and climbed back under the desk. Sophie followed her and Jules disappeared into his tent.

'Would you like to join me for some cocoa, dear?' Digby asked.

'That would be lovely, thank you,' Clarissa replied wearily.

SPECIAL DELIVERY

The next morning the storm had blown away and the sky was a dazzling shade of blue. Clementine, Sophie and Jules slept in until Lavender told them it was time to get up. She made the rounds, pressing her little snout onto the sides of their faces until they stirred.

In the kitchen, Digby Pertwhistle was making tea.

'Hello Uncle Digby,' said Clementine, yawning, as the trio arrived to have breakfast. 'Where's Mummy?'

'She's upstairs talking to Aunt Violet,' the old man said. 'Did you enjoy your safari?'

'It was exciting,' said Clementine, beaming. 'We saw some strange creatures.'

Jules placed three photographs down on the table. He spread them out. Digby laughed.

'Just as well that pig of yours is patient,' he said, marvelling at the pictures. There was Lavender with elephant ears, Lavender with a monkey mask and Lavender wearing a tutu.

'That's a rather unusual animal to find on an African safari,' said Digby, pointing at the one of Lavender in the tutu.

'I thought the tutu might have made her look like a lion but I think she just looks like a ballerina pig,' Clementine sighed.

The doorbell rang.

'I'll get it,' Clemmie yelled and raced out of the kitchen. She almost ran into Aunt Violet and her mother as they reached the bottom of the stairs.

'Good heavens, young lady, you might have killed us,' said Violet, a scowl creasing her face.

'I'm sorry, Aunt Violet. You look nice today,' Clementine said, noticing her great-aunt's white pants-suit and stylish pink shoes.

'Yes, well, I can't say the same for you at the moment.' The old woman shook her head.

Clarissa opened the front door and Clementine skipped across the giant entrance hall to see who was there. A man in a uniform handed her mother an envelope.

'Special delivery for Lady Clarissa Appleby from Cunard's,' the young man announced. 'Please sign here.'

Clarissa scribbled her signature and thanked the fellow, then closed the door.

'What is it, Mummy?' Clementine asked.

'I don't know, but I think we should open it together in the kitchen,' Clarissa smiled.

Violet was standing at the bottom of the stairs looking up at the portraits on the wall.

Clementine stopped and followed her gaze. 'You were lovely.'

'Yes, I was, wasn't I?' The old woman's eyes took on a sparkly sheen.

'Do you want to have some breakfast?' Clementine held out her hand to Aunt Violet.

'Oh, for heaven's sake, I'm perfectly capable of finding my own way to the kitchen – which is where I *presume* we'll be eating, seeing that the dining room is reserved for paying guests,' Violet snapped.

Clementine's lip began to tremble. The old woman caught sight of her and sighed.

'Oh, all right. Come along, Clementine, if it makes you feel better, you can show me the way.'

The old woman reached down and slipped her hand into Clemmie's. There was a spark of electricity between them. 'Oh!' they both gasped in unison. Clemmie giggled and looked up at her great-aunt. She stared at her face, past the wrinkles and the frown lines.

'You know, Aunt Violet, it's funny but we have exactly the same colour eyes, you and me.'

Violet gazed at the child. Her brow furrowed and just for a moment she remembered herself as a young girl and thought she could have been looking into a mirror.

'Well, of course, I am your grandfather's sister, Clementine,' Violet replied. The old woman looked up and caught her niece's gaze. 'Isn't that right, Clarissa?' she said.

Clarissa nodded. 'Of course, Aunt Violet. Now,' she said, changing the subject, 'come along, breakfast's ready.'

'After breakfast you'll have to find Pharaoh for me. He got out last night and he could be anywhere,' Violet informed them.

Clementine gulped. She didn't like the thought of the sphynx lurking about the house.

As Clementine and Aunt Violet followed Clarissa into the kitchen they found Digby, Sophie and Jules huddled together by the back door.

'What *is* it?' Sophie asked, in a confused voice.

'I think it must be that giant rat Clementine was talking about,' Jules whispered.

'Did you say rat?' Aunt Violet strode towards the group. 'That's not a rat, that's my baby.' She stared into the basket and her eyes grew as round as dinner plates. 'Oh, Pharaoh! How could you?' Violet clasped her hand to her mouth.

Clementine ran to see.

'Lavender!' she giggled. 'That's lovely!'

There in the basket, Pharaoh and Lavender were fast asleep. Pharaoh had his paw resting on Lavender's tummy and he was purring like a diesel engine.

'Maybe Pharaoh thinks he's a pig,' Jules said. 'They kind of look the same – except Lavender's much prettier.'

'Wash your mouth out, young man,' Violet rebuked.

'Come and sit down, Aunt Violet, and I'll pour you a cup of tea,' said Clarissa, rolling her eyes at her aunt's theatrics.

'Toast's up,' Digby Pertwhistle called. The children raced back to the kitchen table.

'What did the man deliver?' Clementine

asked her mother, pointing at the envelope that was sitting on the table.

'Oh, I'd almost forgotten about that.' Her mother sat down and picked it up. She ran her finger under the flap and pulled out a letter, which she read aloud. *'Dear Lady Appleby, it is my pleasure to inform you that you are the winner of the Cunard's Coast to Coast Competition.'* Clarissa scanned ahead silently.

'But what did you win, Mummy?' said Clementine, fizzing with excitement.

Sophie looked on beside her friend, and Jules raced over to stand behind Clarissa and read over her shoulder.

'Goodness! It's a cruise. On board the Queen Mary 2, all the way around the world. It's for three whole months!' Clarissa exclaimed. 'I can't go, of course. What about you, Digby?'

The old man pursed his lips and shook his head. 'Couldn't possibly leave you and the little one for that long.'

'I would get seasick,' Jules piped up.

Aunt Violet was on the edge of her seat. 'The Queen Mary 2, you say? When I was a young woman I sailed on the original Queen Mary,' she said. 'With your father and our parents, actually. It was one of the happiest times we ever had as a family.'

Clementine skipped around to the end of the table and pulled on her mother's arm. She whispered something in her ear.

Clarissa gave her daughter a broad smile. 'Yes, I think that's a lovely idea, Clemmie.'

'Aunt Violet,' said Clementine happily, 'would you like to go on a long holiday?'

Violet frowned and looked from Clementine to her niece. 'Really? You'd do that for me, Clarissa?'

Clarissa nodded and handed Clementine the letter, which she took around to her great-aunt.

'That's . . . that's very kind.' Aunt Violet wiped her hand across the corner of her eye.

Clementine smiled at her mother and then at Uncle Digby. He gave her a knowing wink.

'But you can wipe those silly smiles off your faces. Three months is not forever, you know.' Violet sniffed and straightened her shoulders. 'Just you wait and see. I'll be back.'

CAST OF CHARACTERS

The Appleby household

Clementine Rose Appleby	Five-year-old daughter of Lady Clarissa
Lavender	Clemmie's teacup pig
Lady Clarissa Appleby	Clementine's mother and owner of Penberthy House
Digby Pertwhistle	Butler at Penberthy House
Aunt Violet Appleby	Clementine's grandfather's sister

Pharaoh	Aunt Violet's beloved sphynx

Friends and village folk

Margaret Mogg	Owner of the Penberthy Floss village shop
Clyde Mogg	Margaret's husband
Claws Mogg	Margaret's tabby cat
Father Bob	Village minister
Adrian	Father Bob's dribbly bulldog
Pierre Rousseau	Owner of Pierre's Patisserie in Highton Mill
Odette Rousseau	Wife of Pierre and mother of Jules and Sophie
Jules Rousseau	Seven-year-old brother of Sophie
Sophie Rousseau	Clementine's best friend – also five years old
Mintie	Sophie's white kitten

| Poppy Bauer | Clementine's friend who lives on the farm at Highton Hall |

Hotel guests
Mr and Mrs Floyd and Zelda Sparks
Miss Becca Herring
Mr and Mrs Edward and Sandra O'Connell

CLEMENTINE ROSE
and the Pet Day Disaster

Jacqueline Harvey

RANDOM HOUSE AUSTRALIA

For Ian, as always, and for Eden,
who looks a lot like Clementine Rose!

FIRST DAY

Clementine Rose pushed back the bed covers and slipped down onto the cool wooden floor. A full moon hung low in the sky, lighting up pockets of the garden outside and casting a yellow glow over her room. Somewhere, a shutter was banging in the breeze, keeping time like a drummer in a marching band. But that's not what woke Clementine up. She was used to the noises of Penberthy House. It talked to her all the time.

Clementine tiptoed to the end of her bed and knelt down. She rested her head on Lavender's tummy but the little pig was fast asleep in her basket. Her shallow breaths were interrupted every now and then by a snorty grunt.

'I'd better get dressed,' Clementine whispered. 'I don't want to be late on the first day.'

Clementine skipped over to her wardrobe. Hanging on the door was her favourite new outfit. There was a pretty pink and white checked tunic, white socks and red shoes. Clementine especially adored the red blazer with swirly letters embroidered on the pocket. It was her new school uniform, which she had insisted on wearing around the house for the past week. Clementine had packed and repacked her schoolbag for almost a month too.

Clementine wriggled out of her pyjamas and got dressed, buckling her shoes last of all. She brushed her hair and pinned it off her face with a red bow. She smiled at her reflection in the mirror.

'Very smart,' she whispered to herself, just as Mrs Mogg had done when Clementine had appeared at the village store in her uniform the day before. Clementine glanced at her pet, who hadn't moved a muscle. She decided to let Lavender sleep in and headed downstairs to find her mother and Uncle Digby.

On the way, she stopped to chat with her grandparents. Well, with the portraits of her grandparents that hung on the wall.

'Good morning, Granny and Grandpa. Today's that big day I was telling you all about yesterday and the day before and the day before that. I can't wait. I'll get to play with Sophie and Poppy and I'm going to learn how to read and do numbers and tell the time. Did you like school?' She peered up at her grandfather. She could have sworn he nodded his head ever so slightly.

'What about you, Granny?' She looked at the portrait of her grandmother dressed in a splendid gown, with the Appleby diamond tiara on her head. She wore the matching necklace and earrings too. Everyone had thought the jewellery was lost until Aunt Violet had found it when she came to stay. Now the tiara and earrings were safely hidden away in the vault while her mother decided what to do with them; the necklace was still missing. Uncle Digby said that if the jewellery was sold it would bring enough money to pay for a new roof, which Penberthy House badly needed. But Lady Clarissa said that she would wait a while to decide. The roof had leaked for years and they were used to putting the buckets out, so there was no hurry.

Clementine studied her grandmother's expression. There was just a hint of a lovely smile. She took that to mean that she had enjoyed school too.

Clementine looked at the next portrait along, which showed a beautiful young woman. Clementine had called her Grace until, to her surprise, her Great-Aunt Violet had arrived at the house a few months ago and revealed that she was the woman in the painting. Clementine was shocked to learn that the woman was still alive because everyone else in the pictures was long gone.

Aunt Violet and Clementine hadn't exactly hit it off when they first met but for now the old woman was away on a world cruise, so Clementine didn't have to worry about her. Sooner or later, though, she'd be back.

Uncle Digby always said that a day at the seaside would cheer anyone up. So Clementine thought Aunt Violet should be the happiest person on earth by the time she returned from her cruise. When she had told her mother and Uncle Digby that, they had both laughed and said that they hoped very much that she was right.

Downstairs in the hallway, the ancient grandfather clock began to chime. Clemmie always thought it sounded sad.

She counted the chimes out loud. 'One, two, three, four. Mummy will have to get that silly clock fixed. It can't be four o'clock because everyone knows that's in the afternoon. Have a good day,' she said to her relatives on the wall. 'I'll tell you all about school when I get home and maybe, Grandpa, I'll have learned a new poem for you.' Ever since Clemmie could talk, Uncle Digby had taught her poems, which she loved to recite. She often performed for guests who came to stay too, and even though she couldn't yet read, she had a wonderful memory.

Clementine bounced down the stairs and along the hallway to the kitchen. It was still in darkness. Pharaoh, Aunt Violet's sphynx cat, was asleep in his basket beside the stove.

'Mummy and Uncle Digby must be having a sleep-in, like Lavender and Pharaoh,' Clementine said to herself. She hoped they would be up soon.

The little girl climbed onto the stool in the pantry and pulled out a box of cereal, set a bowl and a spoon on the table and fetched the milk from the fridge.

She managed to pour her breakfast without spilling too much. Thankfully, none landed on her uniform.

Clementine listened to the sounds of the house as she ate. Sometimes when people came to stay they asked her mother if Penberthy House had any ghosts. Most children Clemmie's age would have been frightened by the idea, but she often imagined her grandfather and grandmother coming to life at night-time, stepping out of their paintings and having tea in the sitting room, or drifting through the halls.

Clementine swallowed the last spoonful of cereal. 'Good,' she said to herself. 'Now I can go as soon as Mummy and ... Uncle Digby ...' Her eyelids drooped and she yawned loudly.

She rested her head on the table and within a minute she was fast asleep.

TIME
TO GO

'Clemmie.' Lady Clarissa gently stroked her daughter's hair. 'Wake up, sleepyhead.'

Clementine's face crumpled and she struggled to open her eyes until she remembered what day it was and sat bolt upright.

'Did I miss it?' she asked.

'Miss what?' her mother replied.

'School, of course.' Clementine sniffed. She could smell toast cooking.

'No, Clemmie, it's just after seven.' Her mother shook her head. 'How long have you been up?'

'I don't know. The clock chimed four times but it must be broken because that's in the afternoon,' Clementine explained.

'Oh dear, you've been up for hours, silly sausage. I hope you're not too tired for your first day.' Lady Clarissa put a plate of hot buttery toast with strawberry jam in front of her daughter. 'Four o'clock can be in the morning too, Clemmie, and it's very early – at least three hours before you usually get up.'

'Oh.' Clementine frowned. 'Well, today I'll learn how to tell the time and then I won't get up too early tomorrow.'

Digby Pertwhistle arrived in the kitchen. He had been the butler at Penberthy House for longer than anyone could remember and was more like a beloved uncle to Clarissa and Clementine than an employee. He and Clarissa ran the house as a country hotel, but unfortunately guests were few and far between.

'Good morning, Clementine. Are you all ready for the big day?' he asked, his grey eyes twinkling.

'Oh yes, Uncle Digby,' said Clementine, nodding. 'I've been ready forever.'

Digby and Clarissa smiled at one another. That was certainly true.

'Well, eat up your toast and drink your juice. You'll need lots of energy. I've packed your morning tea and I think –' her mother opened the lid of the red lunchbox which had Clementine's name written neatly on the lid – 'Uncle Digby has added a treat.' She snapped the lid closed again.

The old man winked at Clementine. She tried to wink back but she just double blinked instead.

'I've got the camera ready,' said Digby. He walked over to the sideboard and picked up a small black bag.

'Goody!' said Clementine. She finished the last bite of her toast and jumped down from the chair. 'I'll just get Lavender ready. She had a sleep-in.'

'Clemmie, I don't know if we can take her with us today,' said her mother. 'I'm not sure how the school feels about pets.'

'But I told her she could come. Please,' Clementine begged her mother.

Pharaoh let out a loud meow as he stood up in his basket and arched his back.

'No, Pharaoh, you are definitely not coming. Can you imagine what would happen if we took you to town and you got away?' Digby shook his head.

'We don't want to make Aunt Violet cross again, that's for sure,' Clementine replied. 'But Lavender will be so sad if she has to stay home. She's been looking forward to school for as long as I have.'

'Well, what about if I take care of Lavender when you and your mother go into school,' Digby suggested. 'We can go for a walk around the village and I can pop into the patisserie and see Pierre.'

'And you can get a great big cream bun for your morning tea!' Clementine announced.

'Oh, I haven't had one of Pierre's cream buns for ages.' Digby's stomach gurgled at the thought of it.

'All right, now run along, Clemmie, and brush your teeth. We'll have to leave soon,' her mother instructed.

Clementine skipped up the back stairs to her room on the third floor, singing to herself on the way, 'I get to go to school today, I can't wait, hip hip hooray …'

OLD FRIENDS, AND NEW ENEMIES

'Look, Clementine, there's Sophie and Jules,' Lady Clarissa said as Digby Pertwhistle's ancient Mini Minor trundled to a halt outside the school gates. Clementine loved the way the ironwork on the gates was woven together with fancy letters on either side, the same as on her blazer pocket.

Ellery Prep was in the centre of Highton Mill, a short drive from her home in Penberthy Floss. The limestone school buildings nestled behind a neatly trimmed hedge, and several chimney pots poked up into the sky from the slate rooftops. Behind the classrooms and the office there was a large field where the children played at break times. The far end of the ground was bordered by an ancient stone cottage with a rambling garden of creepers and flowers that did their best to invade the school grounds.

'And there's Poppy and Jasper and Lily too!' Clementine leaned forward, craning her neck to see who else was among the group arriving at the gate.

'So, young lady, what do you think you're going to learn today?' Digby asked.

'Everything!' she exclaimed.

'Clemmie, I don't know if you'll learn *everything* on the first day,' Lady Clarissa said. 'You might have to be a little bit patient.'

'But I don't like being patient.' Clementine frowned and shook her head. Lavender grunted as if to agree.

'Oh dear, even the pig knows that's true,' Digby laughed.

'Come on, we'd better get you inside,' said Lady Clarissa as she got out of the car. Clementine hopped out and lifted Lavender off the seat and put her on the ground. Today the little pig was in her best red collar and matching lead.

Digby retrieved Clemmie's enormous backpack from the boot. 'Ready?' he asked.

'Yes. Mummy, can you take Lavender's lead for a minute?'

Digby settled the bag onto Clementine's shoulders. 'You still look like a tortoise, my dear,' he said with a smile, 'but at least now you're part of a family of tortoises.' He gestured towards the growing crowd of new students, whose gigantic bags were almost tipping them backwards.

'Clementine!' Poppy caught sight of her friend and raced towards her. Sophie saw her and rushed over too.

The three girls linked arms and giggled.

Lady Clarissa said hello to Poppy and Sophie and walked over to where their mothers, Lily

and Odette, were standing together talking. Sophie's brother Jules and Poppy's brother Jasper had disappeared inside the school grounds. They were older and knew exactly what to do.

Clementine and her friends were chatting about this and that when Clemmie noticed a boy with wild brown curls. He was standing beside a stout woman with the same brown curls and he was staring at Clementine and frowning.

She waved at him but he didn't wave back. He just kept on staring.

'Who's that boy over there?' Clementine asked her friends.

'Where?' they replied.

'Over there next to the lady with the curly hair. He keeps looking at me.'

'I don't know. I've never seen him before,' Sophie replied.

Poppy shrugged.

It was almost a quarter past nine. All the older students had disappeared into their classrooms and it was time for the new students to meet with Miss Critchley, the head teacher.

Clementine Rose thought that Miss Critchley, a pretty young woman with long auburn curls, was the most beautiful lady she'd ever seen. On the day Clemmie had gone for her interview, Miss Critchley had been wearing a pale pink cardigan with silk roses embroidered around the collar and a pale pink dress with a matching pair of ballet flats. Clementine had decided to ask Mrs Mogg if she could make her a dress just like it.

'Clementine, we have to go in,' her mother called. Lily and Odette beckoned for Poppy and Sophie to join them too.

Clementine nodded at her mother. 'I'll just say goodbye to Uncle Digby and Lavender.' She raced away to where Digby Pertwhistle was standing a little further along the footpath. Lavender had been chomping on a clump of sweet clover growing beside the fence.

'Have a wonderful day, my dear,' said Digby. He leaned down and Clementine wrapped her arms around him and kissed his cheek.

'Thank you, Uncle Digby,' she said, smiling excitedly. Then Clemmie bent down and gave Lavender a kiss on the top of her bristly head. 'Be a good girl for Uncle Digby and I will see you after school.'

Lavender grunted.

'No, you can't come with me, Lavender. Mummy says there's a rule that pigs aren't allowed to go to school.' Clementine sighed. 'I know, it's silly, but I shouldn't break the rules on my first day.' Clemmie then leaned down and whispered into Lavender's ear. 'One day, I'll find a way for you to come.'

'Run along, Clemmie, you don't want to be late. I think I'll go and pay Pierre that visit.' Digby winked at the girl.

Clementine double blinked back at him. She hadn't noticed that the boy with curly hair was still staring at her.

As Digby strolled off, the boy approached Clementine. 'Your dad's a hundred,' he said.

Clementine looked at him and frowned. 'My dad? Oh, you mean Uncle Digby. He's not my dad,' she replied. 'And he's not a hundred. He's seventy-one.'

'Where's your dad, then?' the boy asked.

'He's a mystery,' Clementine replied.

'He's a mystery?' the boy repeated. 'That's stupid. How can a dad be a mystery?'

'I don't know exactly, but mine is,' Clementine replied. She'd never been asked about her father before. Everyone in Penberthy Floss knew that she had arrived at Lady Clarissa's house in the back of Pierre Rousseau's van, in a basket of dinner rolls. It had been an unusual way to join a family, but the adoption papers had all been in order and Clementine had definitely gone to the right home.

Clementine wanted to tell the boy that he was stupid too but then she remembered what her mother and Uncle Digby were always telling her: 'If you can't say something nice, don't say anything at all.'

She kept quiet and rushed off to her mother, except that her tongue poked out at him at the last second. She didn't really mean to. It just sort of happened.

'Well, excuse me, young lady!' The boy's curly-haired mother had reappeared just in time to spot Clemmie's lizard tongue. 'You're a rude little creature, aren't you?'

Clementine felt like a thousand butterflies were having a party in her tummy. And they hadn't been invited.

A NEW
TEACHER

The children and their parents were ushered into the small school hall, which also doubled as the gymnasium. Clementine sat next to her mother with Sophie on the other side and Poppy along further. There were twenty children starting in the kindergarten class. Miss Critchley approached the microphone and welcomed the students and their parents.

Clementine was busy studying the young woman's outfit. Today she had on a dark blue blouse with a bow at the front and a pair of grey pants. Her hair was pulled back softly from her face. Clementine still thought she was the most beautiful lady she'd ever seen.

'Now, I know that some of you might be sitting there with a few butterflies in your tummy,' said Miss Critchley with a kind smile at the group. 'But let me assure you, that's absolutely normal. I imagine you're a little bit nervous and a little bit excited all in one.'

Clementine nodded. So did lots of the other children. Miss Critchley definitely knew a lot about kindergartners, Clementine thought to herself.

'I just need to go through some of the school procedures so that we all know what we're doing and then I will introduce you to your class teacher.'

Clementine wondered if she'd misheard her. Wasn't Miss Critchley going to be their teacher? She didn't want to have anyone else.

'In the afternoon, all of the students will wait for their parents at the school gate under the supervision of a teacher, unless of course you live here in the village. If so, you can walk home and perhaps in the future you might like to ride your bike to and from school ...'

Clementine wasn't listening. She was wondering who was going to be their teacher. The butterflies in her tummy now seemed to be having a boxing match. She didn't like this one bit.

'We encourage parents to come along and help with reading and other activities in the classroom ...'

Clementine's eyes darted around the room, looking for the person who could be their teacher. There was a man in the front row. He had greasy hair and the tail of a dragon tattoo poking out from his shirt sleeve. But then she saw a little girl sitting beside him and guessed he was one of the fathers. There was a lady with blonde hair at the far end. Perhaps it was her.

'And now I'd like to introduce Mrs Ethel Bottomley, who'll be teaching the kindergarten class this year. Mrs Bottomley has many years of experience and is an excellent educator. I know she's looking forward to working with you all.'

Clementine's stomach lurched as she looked up and saw a short woman wearing a drab brown check jacket and matching skirt heading for the microphone. Mrs Bottomley's low-heeled brown shoes clacked on the timber floor and were just about the ugliest things Clementine had ever seen. A helmet of brown curls perched on top of her head and Clementine thought they reminded her of someone else.

'Good morning, parents and children, my name is Ethel Bottomley.' She spoke with a very strange voice. It was whispery but posh at the same time. 'We all know that kindergarten is a very important time in every child's life. It's a time to shake off the playful habits of youth and start some serious study. Rest assured there will be time for fun – orderly fun, of course. And parents, please know that I have high standards and very high expectations. The children will

not be spoiled under my care.' The old woman grinned, revealing a row of yellowed teeth.

Clementine recoiled in her seat.

'But I don't want her,' she whispered to her mother.

'Clementine, I'm sure that Mrs Bottomley is perfectly lovely. You just need to get to know her,' her mother whispered back. But Clarissa felt a little uncertain too. Mrs Bottomley wasn't quite what she had in mind when she pictured her daughter's kindergarten teacher either.

Miss Critchley returned to the microphone. 'Thank you, Mrs Bottomley. Now we should be getting to class, children. Please say goodbye to your parents and follow Mrs Bottomley to the door.'

Clementine felt as if there was a wedge of bread stuck in her throat.

'Goodbye, Clemmie, have a lovely day,' said Clarissa, as she blinked back a tear. She'd been determined not to cry but she hadn't imagined how hard it would be to see her baby starting school.

Clementine clung to her mother. She didn't want to let go.

Sophie reached for her hand. 'Come on.'

'No.' Clementine felt the sting of tears prickling her eyes.

'Clemmie, it's all right,' her friend Poppy tried.

'You have to go, sweetheart. It will be lots of fun,' her mother said. She tried to prise loose Clemmie's arms, which were clamped firmly around her middle.

Arabella Critchley noticed her reluctant student and approached the group.

'Hello Clementine, it's lovely to see you.' She crouched down to meet the child's gaze. Clementine's blue eyes looked like pools of wet ink. 'Do you want to come with me?'

Clementine shook her head.

'I don't know what's got into her,' whispered Lady Clarissa as Miss Critchley stood up. 'She's been looking forward to school for weeks. It's been a battle to get her to wear anything other than her uniform.'

The rest of the class was now standing at the door in two higgledy-piggledy lines.

'Kindergarten, let's see if we can straighten up. Now!' Mrs Bottomley barked.

The children snapped to attention and the lines became perfectly parallel under her outstretched arms.

'Clementine, why don't I take you to class?' Miss Critchley tried again.

Clementine didn't know why she was holding onto her mother. She'd been so excited about school and now Sophie and Poppy were going to start without her.

'Is that little one going to join us?' Mrs Bottomley called from the front of the line. 'Or is she having a bit of a sook?'

'We'll be along in a minute,' Miss Critchley replied firmly. She brushed a rogue strand of hair away from Clementine's face.

Clementine felt silly. She wanted to go with the rest of her class. She didn't want to be last and she didn't want to be called a sook.

'You know, Clementine, on my first day of

school I didn't want to go either. My older brother had told me all sorts of terrible stories and I was scared stiff,' Miss Critchley explained.

'What stories?' Clementine whispered.

'He told me that the headmaster had a secret cupboard full of canes and that he walked around the school whacking children willy-nilly,' said Miss Critchley. 'And you know what? None of it was true. He'd only said it to make me afraid and he succeeded. Is there anything you're afraid of?'

'I thought you were going to be my teacher,' Clementine said, frowning. 'I don't want Mrs Bottom.'

'You mean Mrs Bottomley, Clementine, and I can assure you that her bark is much worse than her bite. She comes across as being a bit stern but she's a big squishy marshmallow underneath,' Miss Critchley explained.

'A big squishy *brown* marshmallow,' Clementine whispered.

'What do you mean?' Miss Critchley asked.

'It must be her favourite colour,' Clementine said.

'Oh,' Miss Critchley smiled. She realised that Clementine was referring to Mrs Bottomley's clothes. 'That's right, you were quite the stylish young lady when you came for your interview and you asked me about my dress.'

Clementine's eyes sparkled and she seemed to perk up.

'Shall we go to class?' The head teacher asked. Clementine released her mother from the vice-like grip and put her hand into Miss Critchley's. They headed for the door.

Suddenly Clemmie ran back and gave Lady Clarissa a final hug. 'Bye Mummy!'

'See you this afternoon, Clemmie, and have a wonderful day,' Lady Clarissa sniffed.

CLASS
TIME

Clementine Rose arrived at her classroom just as Mrs Bottomley was calling the roll and asking the children to stand in alphabetical order at the back of the room.

Poppy was standing beside the curly-haired boy Clementine had seen outside the school.

'Excuse me, Mrs Bottomley,' Miss Critchley interrupted. 'This is Clementine Rose Appleby.'

'Hello dear. You've got over the wobbles, I see. Very good. Appleby. You're first on the roll so you'll need to stand next to Angus up the back there. Angus, put up your hand so Clementine knows who you are.'

The boy with the curly hair raised his hand slightly. Clementine wondered why they had to line up again inside the classroom. There was a lot of time-wasting at school, she decided.

Reluctantly, Clementine walked to the back of the room and stood beside the boy.

Poppy stood on his other side. She leaned around him and asked, 'Are you all right?'

Clementine nodded. She didn't want to talk about what had happened earlier. It made her feel all red.

Mrs Bottomley continued calling names until everyone was standing at the back of the room.

'I have just placed you in what we call alphabetical order. Can anyone tell me what that is?'

A sharp-looking girl with a face like a fieldmouse shot her hand into the air.

'Yes, Astrid,' Mrs Bottomley called.

'It's when you put words into order using the letter of the alphabet that they start with,' the child replied.

'Very good. Now, can anyone tell me if I've put you into alphabetical order according to your first names or surnames?'

Clementine wondered what she was talking about. So did the rest of the class, except for the mouse child who put her hand up again.

'Yes, Astrid.'

'That's easy. It's our surnames, because if it was our first names I'd be standing up there near Angus and Anna but she's at the end of the line because her last name starts with a "W".'

'Goodness me, what a clever little girl you are.' Mrs Bottomley beamed at Astrid. Clementine had no idea what Mrs Bottomley was talking about but she wished she would hurry up and teach her how to read. Surely that would take up most of the day.

'I'd like you to sit next to your partner. Angus, you're sitting with Clementine.' The old woman ushered the pair to the front of the room, where she instructed them to sit down at the first double desk. All of the desks formed neat pairs in neat rows. Clementine wondered if Mrs Bottomley had a thing about lines.

'But I don't want to sit with her,' Angus said and pulled a face.

'Angus Archibald, you'll do exactly as you're told, young man.' The teacher glared at the lad.

Clementine almost felt sorry for him. Just for a moment.

Angus slid into his seat and slumped down, resting his elbows on the desk.

'Was that a pig outside with the old guy?' he mumbled.

'Yes,' Clementine replied quietly.

'Is it *your* pig?' The boy turned and looked at her with his head lying on the desk.

Clementine nodded.

'Where does it live?' he asked.

Clementine started to soften. 'She sleeps in a basket at the end of my bed.'

'Pooh!' the boy scoffed. 'That's so dumb. A smelly pig in your bedroom!'

Clementine couldn't help herself. 'Lavender's not smelly at all. She's smart and she's clean and I love her,' she said sharply.

'You love a pig.' Angus turned around to the boy who was sitting behind them. 'She loves a pig.' He pointed at Clementine and oinked.

Clementine felt hot. The collar of her blazer was prickling her skin and she wanted him to stop.

Angus screwed up his face. 'A stupid pig won't win the pet competition.'

'What pet competition?' Clementine asked.

'It's a secret,' Angus bragged. 'I know all the secrets around here and no smelly pigs will be allowed because Miss Critchley hates them.'

Clementine decided to ignore him but she wondered if it was true. Surely Miss Critchley didn't hate pigs, especially not Lavender. She didn't even know her yet.

Mrs Bottomley appeared at the front of the room. She had a marker pen in her hand and was waving it wildly in the air. 'Now that everyone finally has a seat, it's time that we got on with some work.' She approached the whiteboard and wrote the letter 'A', which Clementine recognised. Her last name started with an 'A'. Finally she was going to learn how to read.

'Now this, my little empty vessels, is where we will begin. Can anyone tell me something they can see in the classroom beginning with "A"?'

Astrid's arm shot up like a spring.

'Yes, Astrid,' the teacher beamed.

'Astrid starts with an "A",' she replied, 'and there's an apple on your desk.'

'So there is.' Mrs Bottomley nodded and wrote two words on the board. 'Yes, what were you going to say, Angus?'

'Angus starts with "A" and so does her name,' he pointed at Clementine. 'Applebum.' The boy burst out laughing. Some of the other children giggled, except for a boy at the back of the room who clucked like a chicken.

Clementine glared at Angus.

'Angus Archibald, you need to find some manners, young man, or you'll be out the door and over to see Miss Critchley,' Mrs Bottomley threatened. 'And as for the rest of you,' she said with a glare that silenced the class, 'settle down immediately.'

The lesson continued until the whiteboard was covered in words, none of which Clementine could read at all. She wondered when the lessons would start properly.

The morning dragged on. They did some colouring in and traced the outlines of words with pencils. Clementine tried hard to stay in the lines but it wasn't as easy as she'd thought it would be. And then when she walked over to sharpen a pencil someone scribbled all over the bottom of her page.

'Did you do that?' she asked Angus as she sat back down.

He shook his head. 'No.'

Clementine got up and walked over to Mrs Bottomley's desk, where the teacher was busy thumbing through a magazine.

'Excuse me, Mrs Bottomley. May I please have a new sheet because someone drew all over the bottom of this one?' Clementine asked.

The teacher looked up and sighed.

'I don't have any spare sheets. And I'm sure that no one *else* drew on the page, did they, Clementine? You just have to learn to be more careful with your work.'

'But Angus did it,' Clementine protested.

'Angus,' Mrs Bottomley called across the room. 'Did you make this mess all over Clementine's work?'

'No,' the boy replied, shaking his head slowly. He blinked innocently.

'All right, thank you.' She turned her attention back to Clementine. 'Now, I know that Angus made a silly comment earlier but he's really a very good boy and I can't imagine that he'd be lying about the worksheet. It's very important, Clementine, now that you're a big girl at school, to always tell the truth. And it's really not nice to be a dibber-dobber, you know.'

'But I am telling the truth,' Clementine retorted.

Mrs Bottomley was not going to back down

any more than Clementine was. 'Did you see Angus draw on your sheet?'

'No, but he did it,' Clementine asserted.

'There is no proof, Clementine, so you'll just have to make the best of it and paste that one into your book the way I showed you. It's a pity that your first piece of work is rather messy but I suppose that's a good lesson to learn about doing your best.'

Clementine felt hot and prickly again.

'When are we going to learn to read?' Clementine asked.

'You've been learning that all morning,' Mrs Bottomley smiled.

'Oh.' Clementine frowned and took her sheet back to her desk. She sat down and opened her workbook and pasted the paper into the front. It looked awful.

Angus leaned over and whispered, 'Guess what? I did it.'

Clementine was shocked. 'Mrs Bottomley, Angus just told me that he scribbled on my page,' she called out.

'Did not,' Angus sneered at her.

'Clementine, you really must stop all these false accusations at once,' Mrs Bottomley huffed. 'You don't want to get a reputation for telling tales on your very first day, do you?'

Clementine finished pasting her page into the book and snapped it shut. She looked at the clock and hoped that it would soon be time for morning tea.

ANGUS

Morning tea time came and went in a blink. Clementine sat with Sophie and Poppy out on the veranda and by the time the girls had eaten their snacks and visited the toilet there was no time left to play.

Clementine had decided that visiting the toilet was very important. Just before the morning tea bell, a girl called Erica had an accident in the classroom. Although Mrs Bottomley didn't fuss, Erica cried and everyone felt sorry for her. That is, except for some of the boys, including Angus, who called her a piddle-pants. Mrs Bottomley told the class that it could happen to anyone.

Clementine didn't like to think it could happen to her. She'd had enough attention from her teacher for one day. She had already decided that she'd try her best to do as she was told and then hopefully Mrs Bottomley wouldn't accuse her of telling lies any more.

After morning tea, Mrs Bottomley made the children copy some numbers from the board and then match them with coloured blocks. Clementine wondered when she would learn how to tell the time.

She avoided talking to Angus and tried not to look at him either. But that didn't stop him being naughty.

Clementine just happened to glance up from her work when she saw that Angus was drilling his finger up his nose. She watched as he removed a large glob of yellow snot. He held it in the air and examined it closely.

Angus noticed her watching him and pulled a face. 'What are you looking at?'

'Nothing,' said Clementine, and went back to her work. That's when Angus did something unforgivable. He wiped his finger on her shoulder.

She let out a squeal. 'Ahh!'

'Clementine Rose Appleby, whatever is the matter now?' Mrs Bottomley demanded.

'Angus just put snot on my uniform.' Clementine's lip began to tremble. Her beautiful clean new uniform now had a disgusting booger on it.

'Come here,' said Mrs Bottomley, rolling her eyes.

Clementine stood up. Angus giggled. The boy behind him called Joshua laughed too.

But this time the girls in the class seemed equally offended and nine pairs of eyes bored into Angus's back.

Mrs Bottomley examined the offending yellow glob. With one swift move she pulled a tissue from the supersized box on her desk

and removed it without so much as leaving a mark.

'All gone, Clementine, nothing to worry about,' she tutted. 'Angus Archibald, you will see me at lunchtime. I think our playground could do with some beautification, which you will be in charge of. That behaviour is completely unacceptable.' The teacher walked over to the lad, who crossed his arms and huffed loudly.

'But,' he whined, 'it was an accident.'

Mrs Bottomley's eyebrows furrowed together like a pair of angry brown caterpillars. 'I don't think so.'

'But, Nan ...' Angus pouted.

The whole class gasped.

'What did you just call me?' Ethel Bottomley's eyes grew round and she stood over him like a giant brown toadstool.

Clementine looked at Angus Archibald and then at Mrs Bottomley. They had the same hair; that was why she had thought Mrs Bottomley reminded her of someone. It was the woman who had been standing out the front with Angus. She must be Mrs Bottomley's daughter.

Angus looked at the forbidding woman in front of him.

'Outside. NOW!' she roared.

The lad scurried out the door and onto the veranda like a naughty dog. The kindergarten class had never been left on their own before. No one quite knew what to do.

Sophie and Poppy left their seats and raced up the front to talk to Clementine.

'He's in big trouble now,' Sophie said.

'But if Mrs Bottomley's really his granny, she can't be all that mad with him. Grandparents have to be nice to their grandchildren,' said Poppy. 'It's in the rules.'

'Are you joking? My grandmamma is fierce and French and half the time I can't understand a word she says. She scares me to bits,' Sophie said.

It was hard to tell what was going on out on the veranda, except when Mrs Bottomley roared like a hungry lion.

'It doesn't sound like he's getting any special treatment,' said Clementine. Her eyes were the size of dinner plates.

'Don't you ever call me Nan in class again, young man, or I will have you out of here before you have time to learn to count to one hundred,' Mrs Bottomley bellowed.

The door opened and everyone scurried back to their seats, like ants before a storm.

'Yes, well,' the teacher said, looking around at the class, 'we might as well be honest about this. Angus is my grandson. But rest assured, while I love him very much, he will call me Mrs Bottomley just the same as everyone else does.' She glared at the lad, whose face was red and eyes were puffy. He sniffled as he skulked back to his desk.

Clementine thought that was a bit beside the point. Who cared if he called her Nan? She was more worried about him getting away with bad behaviour, which up until now he'd proven to be very good at. Angus slumped down in his chair. He wiped his eyes with the back of his hands.

Clementine felt a little bit sorry for him. She decided to see if he would talk to her. Maybe then he wouldn't be so upset.

'Are we really having a pet day?' Clementine asked.

Angus shrugged.

Clementine tried again to be friendly. 'That would be fun, don't you think?'

'Maybe,' Angus said with a sniffle.

Clementine noticed that he was in need of a tissue. She walked over to Mrs Bottomley's supersized box, pulled a couple out and handed them to the boy. He took the tissues from her and blew his nose like a trumpet, then thrust them back at her covered in gooey slime.

'You just don't get it, do you?' Clementine sighed, and then dropped the grotty tissues in the bin. She asked Mrs Bottomley if she could go to the toilet and wash her hands. Angus hadn't even said thank you.

LUNCHTIME

Clementine's tummy grumbled and she was very glad when Mrs Bottomley announced that it was time for lunch. The teacher had the children stand in two straight lines and marched them across the quadrangle. Clementine was quite sure now that Mrs Bottomley had a thing about lines.

Because the kindergarten children took longer to eat their lunch, they arrived at the dining room a quarter of an hour before the other classes. That way they had a better chance of finishing their meal and still having time for a run around in the playground before the afternoon lessons.

'Lunch today is Mrs Winky's special sausages with yummy mashed potato and vegetables,' Mrs Bottomley told the group.

Clementine thought that sounded quite good – she loved her mother's sausages and mashed potato. The children lined up once again and the plates of food were handed over to them.

'It smells nice,' Poppy said as she walked over to a table and sat down.

'No, no, no, Poppy, you must sit where I tell you to,' Mrs Bottomley barked. 'Over there with Clementine and Angus and Joshua. I think it's far better to have the girls and boys mixed together at lunchtime.'

Clementine couldn't believe that she had to sit with Angus again.

She put her plate down on the table and realised that she needed to go to the toilet. She didn't want to leave it until later, just in case she had an accident too.

She whispered to Poppy.

'I need to go too,' Poppy replied.

The girls approached Mrs Bottomley and asked if they could go. The old woman huffed and asked why they hadn't gone at morning tea time.

'But we did,' Clementine protested.

Mrs Bottomley muttered something that sounded like 'weak bladders' and then said, 'I'm not too keen to mop up after anyone else today, so yes, off you go.'

The girls returned just minutes later. Angus and Joshua were sitting at the table grinning at one another like a pair of Cheshire cats.

'What are you smiling at?' Clementine asked as she sat down.

'Nothing.' Angus shook his head.

'Yeah, nothing at all,' Joshua added, which only made Clementine more suspicious.

Clementine pushed her fork into the mashed potato and put it in her mouth.

Poppy did the same.

At exactly the same moment both girls spat their mouthfuls of food all over their plates.

'Yuck!' Clementine couldn't get it out quickly enough. 'That's disgusting!'

Poppy was gagging.

Mrs Bottomley was patrolling the tables and saw their carry-on. 'Girls, whatever's the matter this time?'

'There's something wrong with it,' said Clementine. She pointed at the potato. 'It tastes awful.'

'I'll be the judge of that.' Mrs Bottomley whisked the fork out of Angus's hand and dug it into his mashed potato. She shovelled a generous portion of the creamy white vegetable into her mouth.

'Mmm, delicious,' she said. She looked at Clementine and Poppy. 'There's nothing wrong with this at all.'

'I'm sure there's nothing wrong with *Angus's* food because he wouldn't do anything to his own lunch,' Clementine snapped.

'Are you accusing Angus of tampering with

your food?' Mrs Bottomley stared at her. Even her eyebrows looked sharp.

'He must have put something in it when Poppy and me went to the toilet,' said Clementine. She could feel the hot sting of tears prickling her eyes for the second time that day. She also noticed some sprinklings of what looked like salt all over the floor.

'That would be "Poppy and I", Clementine.' The teacher turned to her grandson. 'Angus, did you put anything in the girls' lunch?'

'No, Na– ... I mean, Mrs Bottomley. I didn't and he didn't either.' Angus pointed at Joshua, who covered his mouth.

'But he's smiling,' Poppy said.

'Don't tell me you're going to get in on this act as well, Miss Bauer? My patience is just about worn through today,' the teacher snarled.

Poppy looked as if she might cry too.

'I saw a lovely chocolate pudding for dessert but that's only for the children who eat up everything on their plates,' said Mrs Bottomley. 'You'd better tuck in, hadn't you?'

She turned to walk away and Poppy pulled a face at her. It wasn't fair.

'What is it?' Clementine demanded, glaring at Angus.

He smiled sweetly. 'What do you mean?'

'What did you put on there?' she asked again.

'I told you, we didn't put anything on it.'

'You're lying.' Clementine wanted to go home. She'd had more than enough school for one day.

Angus and his partner in crime finished their meals and took their plates back to the servery.

'He's horrible,' Poppy said, pushing the salty potato about on her plate.

'They're both horrible,' Clementine said.

The two lads returned to the table with giant servings of chocolate pudding and ice-cream.

'Mmm, yum, this is so sweet,' Angus said with his mouth full. 'Not salty at all.' He smiled at Joshua, who grinned back.

'Yeah, sweet,' Joshua replied, giggling.

Clementine glared at the two boys. She wanted some too.

'Come on, Poppy, bring your plate.' She picked hers up and walked towards the servery.

'But Mrs Bottomley said that we could only have it if we ate all our dinner.' Poppy looked sadly at the two plates that were still full of food.

Clementine was watching as the children at the end of the line put their dinner scraps in the bin. Mrs Bottomley was supervising the drink station, where one of the girls had flicked on the tap to the cordial container and couldn't work out how to turn it off. There was a flood of raspberry crush pooling on the floor and Mrs Bottomley was shrieking for someone to get a towel.

With their teacher and Mrs Winky busy cleaning up, Clementine scraped her plate into the bin, then did the same with Poppy's. She placed the empty plates on the servery and picked up a chocolate pudding for herself and another for Poppy.

'But Mrs Bottomley said we had to eat it all,' Poppy said.

'Mrs Bottomley's not fair,' Clementine replied. 'And I'm hungry.'

Poppy nodded. She was hungry too. The girls headed back to the table, where Angus and Joshua were now showering each other with sprinklings of salt and sugar.

'You didn't eat your lunch,' Angus said. 'I'm telling Nan on you.'

'And I'll tell Mrs Bottomley that you called her Nan again,' Clementine threatened. 'And that you put salt all over our lunch.'

'Yeah, we did,' Joshua admitted, grinning.

Angus elbowed Joshua. 'She loves pigs.'

She narrowed her eyes at him. 'Yes, I do love my pig.'

'*You're* a pig,' Joshua said.

Clementine didn't like being called names. She'd never met anyone like Angus or Joshua and she didn't like the way they made her feel one little bit.

NOT
GOING

'My tummy hurts.' Clementine lay in bed clutching her stomach. Tears sprouted from her eyes and rolled down her cheeks.

'Oh, sweetheart.' Her mother sat down beside her. 'You poor little floss. I can't believe that you're sick and it's only the second day of school.'

Clarissa laid the back of her hand on Clementine's forehead. She didn't seem to have a fever.

But something certainly wasn't right. When Clarissa had met Clementine at the school gate yesterday afternoon she had expected her to be fizzing like a shaken bottle of lemonade, but instead she was flatter than a week-old glass of cola. When she had asked about her day, Clementine said that it was okay. Clarissa was worried. It was as if the child she'd delivered to school that morning had been exchanged for another that she barely recognised at all.

'So what was Mrs Bottomley really like?' Lady Clarissa had asked as they scooted along in the car on their way home.

'Brown,' Clementine had replied.

'Clemmie, there must be more to her than that,' her mother had said. 'Did you have fun with Sophie and Poppy?'

Clementine had nodded but her mouth stayed closed.

'Are you feeling all right?'

Clementine had shaken her head. Fat tears had wobbled in the corners of her eyes and rolled down her cheeks. Lady Clarissa had

watched in the rear-view mirror as Clementine wiped them away.

That night Clementine had picked at her dinner, which was most unusual given that it was her favourite: roast lamb with baked potatoes, beans and gravy.

When Clarissa went to check on Clementine later, she found her sound asleep. Her uniform was strewn all over the floor, not hanging proudly on the wardrobe door as it had been for weeks.

Now Lavender was sitting guard on the floor in a bright patch of morning light and Pharaoh was snuggled in beside Clementine on the bed. Lavender looked as worried as Lady Clarissa felt.

Digby Pertwhistle appeared at Clementine's bedroom door. He knocked gently before entering, carrying a tea tray with two boiled eggs and toasty soldiers.

'Good morning, Clementine. Your mother tells me you're not feeling well,' he said with a frown.

'Do I have to go to school?' Clementine asked between teary hiccups.

Clarissa couldn't remember ever seeing Clementine cry as much. Not even when she was a baby. 'If you're not well, Clementine, I think we'll take you over to see Dr Everingham,' she said. 'Should we do that?'

Clementine nodded.

'I'll call the surgery and make you an appointment.' Digby put the tea tray down on Clementine's desk. 'Oh, and in other good news, Aunt Violet called this morning. She'll be back from her cruise this afternoon and has demanded that I pick her up from the dock.'

Digby grimaced and Clementine pinched her lips together trying not to smile.

He raised his eyebrows. 'It'll be lovely to have the demanding old dragon back again, won't it?'

Clarissa rolled her eyes and shook her head. 'Just what we need. At least this weekend there aren't any guests booked in. I think it would be best if we had some time with just the four of us, to get used to how things will work.'

'How long will Aunt Violet stay?' Clementine asked.

'I suspect she could be with us forever,' said Clarissa. 'She has nowhere else to go. She's not the easiest person to get along with but she is your grandfather's sister and I can't just throw her out on the street. Your grandfather and Aunt Violet were very close once. And I remember that when I was a girl she was jolly good fun. I just hope we can find that Violet again.'

'Under all those barnacles,' Clementine said.

'Yes, Clemmie, underneath all her crustiness,' her mother agreed.

'But she can't have my room,' Clementine said.

'Of course she won't have your room, Clemmie,' her mother replied. 'Why would you even think that?'

'When she was here before, I found her in my room and she said that this was *her* room when she was little and she might like to have it again and make it the way it should be.' Clementine's face crumpled as she spoke.

'Oh, sweetheart, there's no chance of that happening. I'm putting my foot down this time. She's having the Blue Room along the corridor up here, whether she likes it or not,' Clarissa said firmly.

'Hear, hear,' Digby agreed. 'I'd best go and make that call to the doctor.' The old man disappeared from the room.

Lavender was snuffling about on the floor at Lady Clarissa's feet. 'Hello you, why don't you give Clemmie a cuddle and see if you can make her feel better,' the woman said. She lifted the little pig up onto the bedclothes.

Clementine hugged Lavender. Pharaoh began to purr loudly beside her too.

'I'll come and let you know when we're seeing Dr Everingham,' said Clarissa, then kissed the top of Clementine's head. She looked at Clementine's uniform, which she'd hung back up on the wardrobe door the night before. 'Clemmie, is there anything else you're not telling me? Did something happen yesterday?'

Clementine shook her head. She didn't want to talk about Angus or Mrs Bottomley or how the whole day was rubbish. She hadn't learned to read or write or do numbers and she still couldn't tell the time.

After lunch, when she and Poppy and Sophie had gone to play, Angus and Joshua had followed them and wouldn't go away. When the girls had finally agreed to a game of chasings, Angus scared Clementine half to death by hunting her into the overgrown garden at the end of the field and saying that a witch lived there. Then the school caretaker Mr Pickles had crashed into the garden and yelled that the children weren't allowed in there because it wasn't safe.

In the afternoon, Mrs Bottomley had made them all lie down on the floor. She said that she was going to read them a story but then she started flipping through the magazine on her desk and making shushing noises. She told them that they should close their eyes and have a little nap. Clementine felt like a baby. She hadn't had an afternoon nap since she was three.

She hadn't told her mother yet, but she wasn't going back to school. There was no point. She could still see Sophie and Poppy at the weekend and she'd learn more from her mother and Uncle Digby than Mrs Bottomley. On top of that she wouldn't have to worry about Angus and Joshua and all the mean things they did.

She was hoping that Dr Everingham would help her tell her mother that this was for the best.

PLAN
B

Uncle Digby managed to get an appointment first thing. So, just before half past eight, Clarissa and Clementine set off to Highton Mill, where the doctor had his surgery. There was no one else waiting when they arrived.

'Good morning, Lady Appleby,' the receptionist said and then looked at Clementine. 'Hello, you must be Clementine Rose. I'm Daisy.' The pretty young woman smiled at the child. Clementine said hello but didn't smile back. 'How old are you?'

'I'm five,' Clementine replied.

'Have you started school yet?' the lady asked.

Clementine nodded. She hadn't seen this woman before. Usually Mrs Minchin sat in the big chair behind the tall desk.

'Hello, Daisy is it? It was her first day yesterday,' Lady Clarissa volunteered. 'How long have you been working here?'

'Not long. I'm just relieving while Mrs Minchin's on holidays. I usually work over at Highton Hall.'

Clementine walked towards the box of toys in the corner. She could hear her mother and the lady talking but she didn't want to listen.

Dr Everingham's door opened and a tall man with a thick head of grey hair appeared at the entrance.

'Good morning, Lady Clarissa.' He walked into the reception area and looked around. 'Hello Clementine.'

Clemmie looked up from where she was examining a rather dog-eared book.

'You'd better come through so we can see what the matter is,' the doctor said with a friendly smile.

Clementine dropped the book back in the box and stood beside Clarissa. She slipped her hand into her mother's.

Inside the doctor's office was an examination table with a small stool to climb up on, a giant desk and three chairs – one for the doctor and two for patients.

Lady Clarissa and Clementine walked in and sat down.

Dr Everingham closed the door and sat down heavily in his leather office chair. He pushed back and swivelled around to face Clementine. He looked at her intently.

'Now tell me, what seems to be the matter?'

'My tummy hurts,' Clementine replied.

'I see. Can you show me where?'

Clementine touched her stomach in the middle and then on the side and further up.

'Is anything else the matter?' he said as he studied her face for clues.

Clementine shook her head.

'And when did it start to hurt?' he asked.

'At school,' she replied.

'And you only started school yesterday, isn't that right?' he asked.

Clementine nodded.

'I'm afraid, Dr Everingham, that I hardly recognised the little girl I picked up yesterday afternoon,' said Lady Clarissa, frowning.

'Ah, I see,' said the doctor.

Clementine knew that he would understand.

'So, what was school like, Clementine?' he asked. 'Did you have a good day?'

Clementine thought about what she would say. There was a long silence.

'Dr Everingham asked you a question, sweetheart. It's polite to answer,' her mother said encouragingly.

Clementine gulped. She knew that if she told Dr Everingham, he would understand. She had known him since she was a baby – although she couldn't remember all that way back. He'd always been kind. When she had to have needles he was very gentle and always gave her a lolly at the end for being brave.

'It was terrible,' Clementine blurted. 'I hate it and I'm not going back again.' A tear started to form in the corner of Clementine's eye. She brushed it away.

'Oh dear,' the doctor replied. 'That doesn't sound good. Can you tell me what happened?'

Clementine took a deep breath. She started at the very beginning with Angus saying mean things about her father and Uncle Digby. She told him about Mrs Brown Bottomley and all that silly lining up. Then there was the scribble on the bottom of her stencil and how she hadn't learned how to read or tell the time. It was as if someone had opened a floodgate: once Clementine started she couldn't stop.

Her mother sat beside her taking it all in. Now everything made perfect sense.

'Oh dear, that's no good at all, Clementine,' the doctor said when she finally paused. 'And do you think that's why you have a tummy ache?'

Clementine nodded. 'So you need to write a letter to the school telling them that I'm not coming back and I'm going to stay at home and Mummy and Uncle Digby are going to teach me everything instead,' she said firmly.

The two adults exchanged a secret look.

'I'm afraid, Clementine, I can't do that,' the doctor said seriously. 'You have to go to school. It's the law. And besides, I'm sure that things will get better. I'll bet you'll be reading and writing in no time flat. And as for that Angus, he'll have to start behaving himself. His grandmother can't be that silly. Sooner or later he'll do something really revolting and she won't be able to ignore it.'

'But he wiped snot on my uniform!' Clementine wondered how much more revolting he could be. She couldn't believe what she was hearing. Dr Everingham could fix everything. Why wouldn't he just write a note and let her stay home forever?

'I can give you something to help your tummy settle down,' he said. 'But you know the best way to feel better is to go back to school.' He looked at his watch. 'If you hurry, you could still get there in time.'

'But I don't want to go,' Clementine said.

'What about we talk to Miss Critchley and see if she can help?' her mother suggested.

Clementine Rose now knew what that mouse Pharaoh had cornered in the kitchen last week must have felt like. Her mother was on Dr Everingham's side too.

'Clementine, I'm sure that your mother is right. Miss Critchley is a very sensible woman. I should know. She's going to marry my son later this year.' The doctor's eyes twinkled.

'Oh.' Clementine's eyes lit up. She liked the idea of Miss Critchley as a bride. 'Do you think she can really help?' Clementine asked.

'I'm sure she can,' Lady Clarissa agreed. The doctor nodded too.

'What about my uniform?' Clementine asked her mother.

'I packed it into the car just in case,' Lady Clarissa replied.

There was no getting out of it.

'Would you like a jellybean?' The doctor popped the lid off the jar and held it out to Clementine.

She looked at her mother.

'Go on, Clemmie, it might make you feel better,' her mother said.

'And how's that pig of yours?' Dr Everingham asked.

'She's good. But she'll be sad because I told her that I wasn't going back to school any more and that we could stay at home and play. And now she'll just have Pharaoh and he doesn't like playing all that much,' Clementine replied.

'Can you keep a secret, Clementine?' asked the doctor.

'What sort of a secret?' she asked.

'Miss Critchley came to dinner with Mrs Everingham and our son Markus last night and she was telling us about something very special that she's planning for the school,' the doctor explained.

'What is it?' Clementine asked.

'She's going to make the announcement to the students this afternoon,' he said. 'I can't tell you all the details but I think it has something to do with pets and a very important lady.'

'Pets? At school?' Clementine's blue eyes widened. 'So Angus really was telling the truth. He said that we were having a pet competition. But then he wouldn't tell me any more.'

'Something like that,' the doctor said. 'But you won't find out if you don't go to school.'

Surely Dr Everingham wouldn't be playing a trick on her, Clementine thought. Doctors knew everything. And Angus probably knew too because Mrs Bottomley was his granny and she would have told him.

'How about I get your uniform, Clementine, and you get changed in Dr Everingham's spare room?' her mother suggested.

Clementine looked from her mother to the doctor. The older man nodded. 'I think that's a very good idea.'

Clementine took a deep breath.

'All right, but only if we can go and talk to Miss Critchley straight away,' she replied.

'And you have to promise not to tell her what I told you.' Dr Everingham winked at Clementine. 'I don't want to get into trouble with my future daughter-in-law.'

Clementine slipped down from her chair and stood in front of the old man. 'Okay,' she said. 'I won't tell.'

A VERY BIG
ANNOUNCEMENT

D r Everingham was right. About a lot
of things. Clementine and her mother
went straight to the office for a chat
with Miss Critchley. The young woman listened
and nodded and seemed to understand exactly
what Clemmie was upset about. Miss Critchley
asked Clementine and Lady Clarissa to wait
a few minutes before they walked over to
the classroom. She went ahead of them and
by the time they arrived, the children were
all sitting in different spots and there was an

empty chair next to Sophie. Angus was beside another boy called Lester, who was the tallest in the class and seemed to wear a permanent frown on his face.

'Good morning, Clementine,' Miss Critchley greeted her at the door. 'I hear you've been to the doctor. I do hope you're feeling better.'

Clementine wondered why she said that when they had talked about it just a little while ago.

Mrs Bottomley strode over to where Clementine and her mother were standing. 'Well, I hope you're not sick. Kindergarten children are terribly good at spreading germs.' She frowned and a deep line ran down the middle of her forehead. 'I can tell you now that I am not in the mood for a bug.'

'Hello Mrs Bottomley, I'm Clemmie's mother, Clarissa Appleby.' She offered her hand.

The old woman smiled thinly and reluctantly reached out to take Clarissa's hand in hers.

'I can assure you that Clemmie's fine,' Lady Clarissa said as she looked at the teacher, who was dressed head to toe in beige.

'Good morning, Mrs Bottomley. That's a good suit. It would look nice with a red scarf,' Clementine suggested.

Mrs Bottomley didn't take kindly to the child's advice. 'I beg your pardon, young lady. I can't imagine ruining my beige with something as ghastly as red.'

'Oh, I think Clementine's absolutely right, Mrs Bottomley. A splash of red would look lovely,' Miss Critchley said, and winked at Clementine.

The teacher rolled her eyes.

'Look, Clementine, there's a spare spot next to Sophie,' said Miss Critchley, nodding at the empty desk. 'Would you like to sit there?'

Sophie was beaming and Clementine smiled back. 'Yes, please!'

'Bye bye, Clemmie, I'll see you after school.' Her mother gave her a quick hug and the girl ran to sit next to her friend.

'I'll walk you out,' Miss Critchley said to Lady Clarissa. 'And by the way, kindergarten, I have a lovely surprise for you later on at assembly.'

The class began to talk at once. 'Have a good day, Mrs Bottomley,' the head teacher said with a smile at the older woman.

Mrs Bottomley pursed her lips and nodded at Miss Critchley. 'All right, kindergarten, we need to focus.'

That morning, Clementine was astonished to realise that she had learned several words since the day before. When Mrs Bottomley asked for someone to read the sentence the class had written together on the board, Clemmie raised her hand. Of course Astrid raised hers first but this time Mrs Bottomley asked Clementine instead.

Clementine studied the squiggles carefully. 'It says …' She paused and concentrated hard, then read each word separately. '"I can play at school."'

'No, it says …' Mrs Bottomley looked at the board. 'Oh yes, I think you're actually right, Clementine.'

Sophie raised her hand. 'Is Clementine getting a sticker?' she asked.

Mrs Bottomley had just given Astrid three and then one to Angus because he recognised the word 'a'.

'Yes, I suppose so.' The teacher marched over to Clementine and placed a sticker on the collar of her uniform. It had a picture of a star on it and, Mrs Bottomley told her, the words said 'Well done'.

At morning tea time, Clemmie, Sophie and Poppy joined a game of chasings with half the class. Miss Critchley had called by their classroom just before they went out and asked Angus and Joshua if they could help her with some special jobs. They didn't come back to the classroom until after the bell had gone.

Lunchtime was better too. Miss Critchley came along to supervise and said that the children could sit with their friends. Clementine ate every last bite of her spaghetti bolognaise and the iceblock they were given for dessert.

After lunch they had assembly. Clementine was amazed to realise that she'd been so busy all day, she'd forgotten about Miss Critchley's surprise.

The smallest students were sitting on the floor at the front of the hall and the older children sat in rows behind them. The teachers perched on chairs around the edge of the room. Most of them were smiling, except Mrs Bottomley, who was trying to get Angus and the other boys at the end of her row to sit quietly.

Miss Critchley stood at the microphone. 'Good afternoon, everyone.'

'Goo-oodafternoo-ooonMissCritch-ley,' the group chorused in an echoey sing-song, which kindergarten struggled to keep up with.

'I hope you are all enjoying the new school term.'

Lots of children were nodding and smiling. Clementine noticed that most of the teachers were too.

'And I hope that you've settled in and are looking forward to the year ahead. Now, I have a very exciting announcement about a

special day we're going to have next week.'
Miss Critchley smiled at the group. 'I wonder
if anyone would like to guess what we're
doing.'

A sea of hands rose into the air.

'Yes, Jemima.' Miss Critchley pointed to a
girl with brown plaits at the back of the room.

'Is it a kite day?' the child asked.

'I have a kite. It's blue,' a little boy in the
front row called out. Everyone laughed.

Miss Critchley shook her head. 'That's a
lovely idea, Jemima, but no, it's not a kite day.'

Hands shot back up again.

'Yes, Dougald.' She pointed at a boy in the
middle of the group.

'Is it a cake stall?' he asked.

'My daddy makes cakes,' Sophie called and
then put her hand over her mouth and giggled.

'He certainly does, Sophie,' Miss Critchley
said. 'And they're delicious. But it's not a cake
stall, although I think there might be some
cakes on the day.'

Clementine raised her hand.

'Yes, Clementine,' said Miss Critchley with an extra-big smile.

'Is it a pet day?' Clementine asked.

'Hey, I told her that!' Angus yelled.

Mrs Bottomley glared at the boy and pulled sharply on his shirt collar.

Angus wrinkled his nose at his grandmother.

Lots of children began calling out about their pets. 'My dog's called Buster ... I've got a cat and he's called Nero ... my goldfish is the fastest swimmer ever ...'

'Settle down, everyone,' Miss Critchley commanded. 'Do you want to know if Clementine is right?'

The whole group nodded like performing seals.

'Yes, we're having a pet day.' Miss Critchley grinned at the excited group. 'On Monday. And there will be a whole lot of different competitions. Cutest pet, best dressed, most unusual, best tricks and lots more. We're supporting a charity called Queen Georgiana's Trust for the Protection of Animals. I'm sure that many of you know our wonderful queen is a lover of all creatures great and small. Through her trust she raises money to help look after abandoned pets. To enter your pet in the competition you'll have to bring a gold coin donation, which we will give to the trust.'

The children were squealing with excitement.

'Goodness, please calm down, everyone. I know it's terribly exciting,' called Miss Critchley.

'It's ghastly,' Mrs Bottomley muttered under her breath.

A small boy in the front row put up his hand.

The head teacher nodded at him. 'Yes, Riley.'

'Does it have to be a dog or a cat?' he asked.

'No, not at all. I know that some of you have quite unusual pets so I'm looking forward to seeing them all,' Miss Critchley replied.

Clementine was relieved to hear this. Surely she'd be able to bring Lavender.

Another hand went up.

'Yes Fergus,' she said, looking at a large lad at the back of the room.

'Can I bring Esteban?' he asked.

Miss Critchley raised her eyebrows. 'May I ask what Esteban is?'

'He's a python,' Fergus replied. 'But he's not poisonous.'

'I don't see why not, as long as he has a cage,' Miss Critchley nodded. 'And he's in it.'

Fergus had a smile from one ear to the other.

'But I don't like snakes,' Poppy said loudly.

Angus glared at her. 'Snakes are cool. And it will bite you because snakes don't like girls.'

'No, it won't,' Poppy retaliated.

'Angus Archibald!' shouted Miss Critchley. Her face was fierce. 'That wasn't nice at all. Please apologise to Poppy for frightening her.'

Angus gave Poppy a sulky 'sorry'. He looked as if he might cry. Mrs Bottomley looked cross.

There were more hands up.

'And I have another surprise,' Miss Critchley announced.

The front row of kindergarten children suddenly sat up straighter, as if a puppeteer was hovering above them and pulling their shoulders with invisible strings.

'We are very fortunate that Queen Georgiana herself will be here to judge the competition.'

The whole hall erupted with excited murmurs.

'All right, everyone. Settle down. There will be a note this afternoon with more details.'

'Mummy, I got a sticker.' Clementine beamed as she met her mother at the school gate and thrust her blazer lapel towards her. 'And Dr Everingham was right. Pet Day is next Monday and Lavender can come to school *all* day.'

Lady Clarissa hugged Clemmie tightly and planted a kiss on top of her head. 'It's nice to have my real daughter back again. I'm glad we got rid of that grumpy little imposter.'

'I love school, Mummy,' Clementine said.

'Well, I'm very pleased about that. You'd have been bored out of your mind if you had to stay at home with Uncle Digby and me for the rest of your days.' She could hardly believe the difference a day made. 'Guess who's back at home?' she asked.

'Aunt Violet?' Clementine guessed.

Lady Clarissa nodded. 'That's right. Shall we pop into Pierre's and get a lovely cake for afternoon tea? She might need some sweetening up.'

Clementine giggled. Her mother was probably right.

AUNT VIOLET

Clementine raced along the hallway and into the kitchen.

'Uncle Digby, Lavender, I got a sticker,' she called, grinning proudly.

Digby Pertwhistle was in the kitchen making a pot of tea. Clementine almost collided with him as he turned from the bench.

'Steady on, young lady,' Digby smiled at her. Clementine wrapped her arms around his middle. 'Sounds like school was much improved today.'

'Yes, it was wonderful. I got a sticker and we're having a pet day too,' Clementine fizzed.

Digby leaned down and whispered into Clemmie's ear. 'You might want to say hello to your Aunt Violet. She's sitting at the table.'

The child released the old man from her grip and ran towards Aunt Violet, who was surveying the scene with her crimson lips pursed.

'Hello Aunt Violet.' Clementine noticed that she was wearing a very stylish blue top over a pair of crisp white linen pants. 'I like your outfit. Did you have a good holiday?'

'Yes, it was … splendid, actually,' the old woman said, as if she was surprised by her own answer.

'That's good. I hoped you'd come back in a better mood than when you left,' Clementine said.

Uncle Digby coughed.

'I mean, I hoped that all that time in the sea air would make you feel happier,' Clementine tried again.

'Really?' Her great-aunt shot her a frosty stare. 'Am I not a picture of contentment?'

Clementine wasn't sure what she meant but she nodded anyway.

'Pharaoh's been a good boy and he and Lavender love each other so much. You know they sleep in the same basket almost every night, except when Pharaoh sleeps down here in front of the stove. Sometimes he curls up on my pillow and he cuddles me,' Clementine prattled.

'Yes, well, he can come back to the Rose Room now,' Aunt Violet commented.

'But Mummy said that you're having the Blue Room up near me,' Clementine replied.

Lady Clarissa entered the kitchen. She'd been dragging Aunt Violet's luggage upstairs. The woman seemed to have enough clothes to start her own department store.

Aunt Violet looked at her niece. 'Is that true, Clarissa?'

Clarissa straightened her shoulders and looked her aunt right in the eye. 'I'm afraid,

Aunt Violet, that I need the Rose Room for paying guests. It's the best by far and the one I use to advertise the hotel. The Blue Room is perfectly lovely too and I've just bought a new duvet for your bed.'

'I don't know why you have to open *our* home to strangers,' the old woman scowled.

'Unless you'd like us all to be living in a tent on the Penberthy Floss Fields, that's something you're just going to have to get used to,' Clarissa replied. She looked towards Digby. He winked at her.

'But I don't want to share a bathroom,' Violet moaned. 'It's not ... It's not civilised.'

'I'm afraid it's something we all have to do,' Clarissa replied. 'And it's hardly a great sacrifice.'

'But I'll have to share my bathroom with ...' She paused and then sneered, 'the child.'

'It's all right, Aunt Violet. I don't take very long in there because I don't like the bathtub very much. It prickles my bottom. Mummy says that if she wins another bathroom makeover she'll get it fixed up but who knows when that will happen.'

Everyone knew about Lady Clarissa's love of competitions. She entered loads of them and had an uncanny knack for winning too. Over the years she'd won everything from a new car to a kitchen makeover, white goods and most recently a three-month round-the-world cruise, from which Aunt Violet had just returned.

'Well, I suppose the Blue Room will have to do,' Aunt Violet huffed.

'It will be fun, Aunt Violet,' Clementine commented. 'I can come and visit you with Lavender.'

'For heaven's sake, don't bring that pig anywhere near me, or my room,' Aunt Violet retorted.

'But if you get to know her, I'm sure that you'll love Lavender as much as I do, and Pharaoh adores her.' Clementine leaned down under the table. 'I think she likes you anyway,' she said, popping her head back up, 'because she's under your chair.'

Aunt Violet's feet shot off the floor so her legs stuck straight out.

'Remove the pig this minute!' she demanded.

Clementine put a finger to her lips. 'Shh. Lavender's asleep and she doesn't like being woken up when she's having her afternoon nap. She doesn't bite, you know.'

Aunt Violet simply said 'hmmph' and turned to Pharaoh, who was preening himself at the back door. 'Come here, precious,' she called.

Pharaoh strolled across the kitchen floor, stopped at Aunt Violet's feet and stared up at her.

Aunt Violet relaxed her ridiculous pose and patted her lap.

Pharaoh studied his mistress for another moment. Then he flicked his tail and padded to the other side of the table where he leapt into Clementine's lap. He nuzzled her face and began to purr like a sports car engine.

'I see,' Aunt Violet harrumphed. 'That's where I stand these days.'

'He always sits in my lap at afternoon tea

time,' Clementine said. The cat kneaded her legs like bread dough before finding a comfortable position.

'I hope you haven't brainwashed him to forget me,' Aunt Violet said.

Clementine frowned. She'd never heard of anyone washing their brain before. 'Are you going to bring him to the pet day?' she asked. 'I'm taking Lavender and I'm going to enter her in everything.'

'I hardly think so.' Aunt Violet shook her head. 'Pharaoh's far too precious to mix with the village riffraff.'

'But we're giving the money to Queen Georgiana's animals.'

At the mention of Queen Georgiana's name, Violet's ears pricked up. 'Will she be there?'

'Oh, yes. Miss Critchley said that she's coming to judge the competition,' Clementine replied. 'That was part of the big surprise and the reason we have to have the pet day so soon.'

'Fancy that,' said Uncle Digby. 'You've always

wanted to meet her, haven't you, Miss Appleby. Didn't you invite her to a party once?'

Aunt Violet eyeballed him. 'Of course not, Pertwhistle, don't be so ridiculous.'

'I can't wait to meet her,' said Clementine. 'I'm going to practise my curtseys. And I'm going to teach Lavender how to curtsey too.'

'What a lot of nonsense,' Aunt Violet snapped. 'Now hurry up and pour that tea before it's stone cold.'

Lady Clarissa exchanged a puzzled look with Digby.

'So,' said Aunt Violet before either of them could speak. 'You must tell me, Clarissa, are there any ghastly guests booked in to stay here over the weekend?'

SCHOOL DAYS

The rest of the week whizzed past and Clementine continued to enjoy her days at school. Poppy and Sophie and Clemmie spent lunchtimes playing games on the field. Even Angus seemed to be better behaved, although he and Joshua did spend a lot of time helping Miss Critchley with jobs. One lunchtime, Angus tried to convince Clemmie that Queen Georgiana hated pigs, but she decided it was best not to believe him.

Every night, Clemmie brought home a reader

and would practise at the kitchen table with Uncle Digby or her mother. She had even convinced Aunt Violet to listen to her one evening.

'Seriously, that must be the most boring tripe I've ever heard, Clementine. Can't you bring home some proper stories?' the old woman had complained before trotting off to the library. She'd returned with a dusty book called *A Little Princess*, by Frances Hodgson Burnett.

Clementine had asked if she was going to read it to her.

'Heavens, no.' Aunt Violet had shaken her head. 'But this is what you should be aiming to read. A proper story.'

The book had sat on the kitchen sideboard for the rest of the week, just begging to be opened.

On Saturday afternoon, Lady Clarissa and Digby Pertwhistle were busy attending to three guests who had booked in for the weekend at the very last minute. Clementine and Lavender were in the kitchen having a snack when Aunt Violet appeared.

'Hello Aunt Violet,' Clementine smiled at her.

The old woman was dressed in a smart pair of navy pants and a white blouse.

Clementine studied her outfit. 'You look nice.'

'Yes, well.' Aunt Violet considered Clementine's own choice of a pretty pink dress with white polka dots. 'Your dress is ... sweet.'

'Thank you, Aunt Violet,' said Clementine.

Aunt Violet went to the sink, filled the kettle with water and popped it on the stove.

'Grandpa's glad that you're here,' said Clementine, looking up from her chocolate brownie.

Aunt Violet spun around. 'Clementine, that's nonsense. Your grandfather has been dead for years and I'm sure that he couldn't care less whether I'm here or not.'

Clementine shook her head stubbornly. 'That's not true. I was talking to Granny and Grandpa this morning and they are both very happy that you're home.'

Aunt Violet seemed puzzled. 'Do you really think so?'

'Oh, yes.' Clemmie's head jiggled up and down.

Aunt Violet finished making her tea, carried it over to the table and sat down.

Clementine slipped off the chair and returned to the table clutching the book Aunt Violet had left on the sideboard.

'Could you read to me?' She stood in front of the old woman, looking up at her piercing ink-blue eyes.

Aunt Violet shooed her away. 'I'm busy, Clementine.'

'No, you're not. You're having a cup of tea,' Clementine insisted. 'That's not busy.'

'Well, I don't want to then,' Aunt Violet snapped.

Clementine's eyes began to cloud over.

'Oh, for goodness sake, it's nothing to cry about.' Aunt Violet placed the teacup down on the saucer with a thud. 'Give it to me.' She snatched the book from Clementine's hand.

'And sit down there.' She pointed at the seat next to her.

Clementine scurried up onto the chair. Pharaoh had made himself comfortable in the basket in front of the stove, where it was toasty and warm. Lavender hopped up from where she was sitting under the table and waddled over to join her friend.

Violet Appleby opened the book and scanned the inscription on the first page.

To our dearest Violet,
On the occasion of your sixth birthday,
Your loving Mama and Papa
xoxo

Something caught in Aunt Violet's throat and she turned the page before Clementine could see what she was looking at. She began to read.

Clementine sat wide-eyed as her great-aunt turned the pages and the story came to life right in front of her. Neither of them realised that a whole hour had passed.

Lady Clarissa appeared in the kitchen carrying an empty tea tray.

'Hello, what do we have here?' she enquired.

Aunt Violet snapped the book shut.

'Please don't stop, Aunt Violet,' Clementine begged.

'I have things to do, Clementine. I can't sit around here all day, can I?' The old woman stood and strode out of the room.

Clementine was confused. 'Did I do something wrong?' she asked her mother.

'No, Clemmie,' Lady Clarissa said, shaking her head. 'Aunt Violet can be a bit of a puzzle, that's all.'

Clementine nodded. 'She's much harder to work out than the ones we do at school.'

PET
DAY

'Are you *really* not coming with us, Aunt Violet?' Clementine asked her great-aunt at breakfast on Monday morning. 'It's not too late to enter Pharaoh in a competition.'

Violet looked up from the toast she was buttering. 'No Clementine, I won't be attending and neither will Pharaoh,' she said firmly.

Lady Clarissa glanced at the clock on the kitchen wall. 'Clemmie, you'd better run up and get Lavender ready,' she advised. 'We'll be leaving in half an hour.'

'She's so excited, Mummy. I'm taking her tutu and ballet slippers for the dress-up competition,' Clementine babbled.

Aunt Violet rolled her eyes. 'I almost feel sorry for the ridiculous creature. A pig in a tutu is too, too much.'

Clarissa laughed at her aunt's accidental joke.

'Oh no, Aunt Violet, Lavender loves to dress up. Mrs Mogg makes her clothes too,' said Clementine. She gave her mother a quick hug and sped off down the hallway.

'Are you sure you won't come along?' Lady Clarissa asked her aunt. 'It's bound to be lots of fun.'

'No, I'd rather eat cold brussels sprouts,' Aunt Violet said with a shudder.

'Well, if you change your mind, you're very welcome.' Clarissa stood up to clear the breakfast things. Digby Pertwhistle arrived in the room carrying a feather duster and cloth.

He'd been up early to get a head start on some of the housework. 'You're coming, aren't you?' Clarissa asked the old man.

'I wouldn't miss it for the world. Clemmie's so excited and I think Queen Georgiana's fabulous.' He winked at Aunt Violet.

Aunt Violet glared back.

An hour later the house was strangely silent. Aunt Violet was rattling around in her room when she decided to make herself some tea. As she descended the stairs she noticed a small black bag on the floor in the entrance hall. She marched over to pick it up and saw some pink tulle poking out.

She opened the bag to have a better look and found a pink collar and lead and a floral garland among the tiny tutu and four ballet slippers.

'Urgh, it belongs to the pig,' she exclaimed. She stuffed the contents back inside the bag and placed it on the hall table.

A moment later, a loose window shutter banged upstairs and Aunt Violet leapt into the air. She looked up towards the noise and locked eyes with her brother – or at least, the portrait of him hanging on the wall.

'What are you looking at, Edmund?' She didn't like the way his eyes seemed to be following her. 'No, I'm not going,' she said decisively.

Aunt Violet shook her head. Obviously she'd been spending too much time with the little one, who believed that the portraits could speak to her. And besides, she was far too busy to go running into town for a silly pet show.

Aunt Violet stalked off to the kitchen to make her tea. But all the while there was a gnawing feeling in her stomach. She caught sight of the book she'd been reading with Clementine. She'd forgotten how much she had loved that story. She smiled to herself as she recalled sitting with her mother on the veranda many years ago. They'd been reading the exact same book and Violet's beloved little terrier Hinchley was curled up on her lap. How she had loved that dog.

'Oh, all right, I'm going,' she muttered under her breath, before removing the kettle from the stovetop. She scurried up the back stairs to her bedroom, where she retrieved her handbag and car keys. Coming down the main stairs, she spotted Pharaoh through the double doors to the right. He was lying on the sitting room floor, basking in a shard of sunlight.

Aunt Violet looked back at her brother. 'Are you happy now?' She picked up the bag from the table. Checking that she had her house keys, the old woman strode to the front door. Her shiny red car was parked in the turning circle. She locked the house, walked over to the vehicle and opened the driver's side door before she realised that she'd left her sunglasses on the dresser in her bedroom. Aunt Violet sighed deeply and shook her head, tutting at herself.

She headed back inside, leaving the door ajar. As she climbed the stairs, she didn't notice a grey streak race out the door and towards the car.

Within a minute, Aunt Violet was speeding towards Highton Mill, the black bag on the passenger seat and her sunglasses perched on her nose.

THE BIG
MOMENT

'And who do we have here?' Queen Georgiana asked Clementine. She smiled at Lavender. The pig looked up at the old woman and seemed to smile back at her. The Queen was currently judging the Cutest Pet category inside the school hall. Queen Georgiana's lady-in-waiting, a stout woman of advanced years, was following closely behind. The woman wore a suit like those preferred by Mrs Bottomley and she had a snarl on her face to match.

Clementine curtsied just as Miss Critchley had taught the girls, and then replied, 'Her name is Lavender, Your Majesty, and she's a teacup.' Clementine giggled. 'I mean a teacup pig.'

'And so she is.' Queen Georgiana reached out to give Lavender a scratch behind the ear. 'And a very pretty little piggy you are too.' Lavender sniffed the Queen's hand before giving her finger a nibble. 'Oh, you cheeky thing,' she gasped and laughed loudly.

Her lady-in-waiting screwed up her nose and whispered under her breath, 'How ghastly. A pig!'

Queen Georgiana's ears pricked up. So did Clementine's.

'For heaven's sake, Mrs Marmalade, this piggy is so clean you could eat your dinner off her belly.'

Clementine smothered a giggle as she imagined Lavender acting as the Queen's dinner plate.

Mrs Marmalade sniffed and muttered a half-hearted apology to Clementine.

The Queen continued along the line. Sophie was standing beside Clementine and holding her cat Mintie, who was wriggling like a garden worm. Sophie curtsied too and almost lost her grip on the ball of white fur.

'If I were you, dear, I'd pop her into that cage there,' the Queen suggested, 'before she gets away. I don't like the look of that dog over there one little bit.' She nodded towards a giant mastiff who was drooling all over the floor. Standing beside the dog was its owner, Angus, who had a very loose grip on the lead. 'I don't know if that boy would be strong enough to hold the pup if something took his fancy.'

Sophie nodded. She wanted to say something but the words just wouldn't come out.

The Queen looked at the silent girl closely. 'Are you all right?'

Sophie nodded again.

'I don't bite, you know,' the Queen grinned.

Sophie nodded for a third time and was very cross with herself.

There were only a couple more pets at the

end of the line, including Esteban, Fergus's python. When Queen Georgiana reached him she stooped lower to make eye contact. Mrs Marmalade stepped away from the creature with a look of horror.

'Good grief, Marmalade, it's a python not a viper. Cute as a button too.' The Queen touched the serpent on the end of his scaly nose.

Fergus grinned broadly.

Mrs Marmalade shuddered.

The Queen concluded her inspections and moved over to confer with Miss Critchley, who was holding a blue ribbon.

There was a lot of nodding and smiling between them before Queen Georgiana took the microphone. 'It gives me great pleasure to announce that the Cutest Pet at today's Ellery Prep Pet Day is …' There was a long pause as the Queen cast her eye over the entrants one last time.

The audience members all held their breath.

'I must tell you that it was a terribly difficult decision and if I had my way everyone would take home a ribbon,' said Queen Georgiana, smiling at the children.

The audience exhaled, as if a room full of balloons had been let down at once.

'But, alas, there can only be one winner.' The group breathed in again. 'And today that title belongs to ... Mintie the lovely little white cat.'

Everyone clapped. Sophie couldn't believe it. Her jaw dropped and her mouth gaped open like a stunned cod. She had been quite sure that Lavender would win.

'Sophie, close your mouth,' her father Pierre called from the audience, 'or you will catch some flies.' Everyone laughed.

Clementine smiled at her friend, and then leaned down and gave Lavender a pat. 'There's still the Best Dressed,' she whispered. 'And you'll look beautiful in your ballet slippers.'

Queen Georgiana strode over to Sophie, who was busy pulling Mintie out of her cage. The Queen pinned the oversized rosette onto the cat's collar. Mintie immediately started tearing at it with her teeth. Flashes were going off as Pierre snapped pictures of his daughter and her prize-winning cat standing next to the Queen.

'Would you like to say anything, dear?' Queen Georgiana held out the microphone to the astounded child.

Sophie could only manage to shake her head.

'I see the cat's still got your tongue.' Queen Georgiana winked at Sophie.

Mintie meowed loudly. It sounded rather like 'thank you'. The audience giggled.

Sophie's cheeks turned bright red.

'Thank you, Your Majesty,' she whispered.

'You're very welcome, my dear. Now put that kitty away again quick smart.' The Queen glared at Angus and his hound, who had moved to the front row. She wondered if he was entered in the next category: Dribbliest Pet.

Meanwhile, outside, Aunt Violet screeched to a halt at the front gate. She gathered up the black bag on the seat beside her and opened the driver's door, failing to see the 'No parking' sign right beside her car.

'Silly child would forget her head if it wasn't screwed on,' she tutted under her breath.

Digby Pertwhistle was outside helping set up the morning tea. He spotted the old woman exiting her car and scurried to meet her.

'Good morning, Miss Appleby, I see you changed your mind.'

'No, I did not.' Aunt Violet peered over the roof of her expensive red car. She didn't notice the shadow that scurried underneath the vehicle.

'May I ask what you're doing here then?' said the old man.

'I have this.' Aunt Violet held the bag aloft. She slammed the car door.

'Oh, it's very good of you to bring Clementine's bag. I don't think she realised that it was missing. But you can't park here,' he said, pointing at the sign.

'Pooh! I'll only be a minute,' she said, waving her hand at him.

'Well, I can take the bag for you and then

you don't need to come in at all,' Digby offered.

Aunt Violet shook her head. 'No, I'll take it myself.' She pursed her lips together tightly. 'I want Clementine to understand that she has to be more careful with her things. She can't expect someone to rescue her every time she's careless.'

'Oh,' said Digby. 'Of course. She is five, after all. I don't suppose it has anything to do with you wanting to meet Queen Georgiana?'

'Of course not,' Aunt Violet snapped.

'You're not even a little curious?' Digby teased.

'No.' She shook her head.

'Well, I think you'll find Clementine over in the hall with the rest of the children. The Best Dressed category will be coming up soon. Then you might like to stay for morning tea – after you've moved the car, of course.'

Violet ignored Digby's last comment and marched through the gates. She almost bumped into Clementine and Lavender, who were on their way to the classroom to get ready. Mrs Bottomley was leading the group – in a straight line, of course. Her mouth was pinched and her eyebrows looked crosser than ever. She was not enjoying Pet Day one little bit, although the layered sponge cake she'd made for the event had been a great triumph, so she had that to look forward to at morning tea.

'Aunt Violet!' Clementine exclaimed. 'I'm glad you changed your mind.'

'I did no such thing,' the woman snarled. She held the black bag aloft. 'You forgot this.'

'Oh, thank you for bringing it. Otherwise we would have missed out.' Clementine smiled at her great-aunt. She hadn't even realised that the bag was missing.

'Well, yes, you need to be more careful in future, Clementine. I can't go running around after you at the drop of a hat,' said Aunt Violet. She looked as if she had just sucked a lemon.

'Thank you, Aunt Violet,' Clementine said again. 'Are you going to stay for the judging?' Clementine asked.

'No, I'm going home to make another cup of tea. The one I was trying to make when your grandfather scolded me about your bag will be stone cold,' Aunt Violet replied.

'Did Grandpa talk to you too? That's so exciting!' Clementine gushed.

'No, of course he did not talk to me,' said Aunt Violet. 'I didn't mean it like that at all.'

But Clementine knew there was something more. She gave Aunt Violet a wave and skipped along with Lavender beside her on the way to the classroom.

Inside the hall, there were peals of laughter as Queen Georgiana announced the winner of the Dribbliest Pet category.

It was a tie. Father Bob had kindly loaned his bulldog, Adrian, to Eddie Whipple, a six-year-old lad from Penberthy Floss. The other winner was Angus's giant mastiff, Martin. The Queen was calling for a mop to clean the stage before the next category, Best Dressed.

Aunt Violet was drawn towards the noise and wondered what on earth was going on. She poked her head into the back of the hall and watched as Her Majesty directed the school caretaker, Quentin Pickles, who was slipping and sliding all over the place.

'Come on, man.' Queen Georgiana pointed at a pool on the stage. 'You missed a bit just there.' The audience was hooting.

'Oh, for goodness sake, give it to me.' Her Majesty wrestled the mop from Mr Pickles, whose face had turned a stony white.

'But, Ma'am, you're the Queen. You can't mop floors. That's my job,' the old man protested, clutching the mop back to his chest.

'Yes, you're quite right. I am the Queen, so I can jolly well do anything I please.' Queen Georgiana flashed him a cheeky grin.

The parents and children wondered if they were watching a pantomime.

Violet Appleby pursed her lips. Could this really be the Queen? The very same woman she had invited to her birthday party when they were girls, and from whom she never received a reply?

Outside, Digby and Pierre were putting the finishing touches to the morning tea. A row of trestle tables heaved under the weight of cream buns, chocolate eclairs, sponge cakes and a scrumptious selection of biscuits and slices. Most had been supplied by Pierre, with some additions from the parents and teachers.

'Well come on, Pierre,' Digby called to his friend. 'We should be getting in. I think Clementine and Lavender are about to be judged.'

The two men placed a long gauze cover over the tables and headed inside.

Clementine Rose and Lavender – now in her costume – followed Mrs Bottomley around to the side entrance of the hall.

'Okay, Lavender, just do your best.' Clementine reached down and gave the little pig a scratch behind the ear. She walked across the stage and was joined by a whole line of children and their pets, which were dressed in a range of outfits. There was a West Highland terrier in a sailor suit, a bunny dressed as a bellhop and, of course, Lavender in her tutu. Poppy was there too with one of the barn cats from their farm. It was a large tabby called Jezabel, dressed in a bride's outfit that Poppy had borrowed from one of her dolls. Jezabel did not look as if she was enjoying the experience one little bit.

'Oh my,' Queen Georgiana gasped as she surveyed the group in front of her. 'Don't you all look gorgeous?'

She walked up and down the line, greeting the pets and their owners. Digby slid into a seat next to Lady Clarissa. He glanced around and saw Aunt Violet standing at the back of the hall. He motioned for her to come and sit down but she ignored him completely.

After a short deliberation, Queen Georgiana again took the microphone from Miss Critchley to announce the winner.

'It gives me great pleasure to award the Best Dressed pet to ... Lavender, the little teacup pig.' She smiled at Clementine, who beamed back at her.

'That's our girl,' Digby called from the back of the hall. Everyone clapped and laughed.

Queen Georgiana passed the microphone back to Miss Critchley and proceeded to pin the blue rosette onto Lavender's tutu. The little pig nibbled Her Majesty's finger and Clementine curtsied.

DISASTER

'Well,' Miss Critchley began, 'I can't believe it's time for our final category: the Pet Most Like its Owner.'

All of the students and their pets, other than those entered in the last section, were now jammed in together at the front of the hall with parents and friends sitting on the rows of seats behind.

'I love this part of the competition,' Miss Critchley beamed. 'It's always a lot of fun.

So, without any further ado, here are the entrants.'

The children and their pets filed across the stage. Among them were a girl from the fourth grade with blonde curls and her equally blonde curly-haired poodle; a lad from the sixth grade with slicked back hair holding a large skink in a terrarium; and a kindergarten boy with rather large ears, who was leading a basset hound. Another boy was wearing a dalmatian costume and holding the most adorable dalmatian puppy. Queen Georgiana was grinning broadly as she tried to decide on a winner.

No one noticed the unusual creature that had slunk onto the side of the stage. He padded along behind the group and emerged in the middle, between a girl with a guinea pig and a lad with a ferret.

The creature looked out at the audience with a sneer on its face.

Queen Georgiana caught her breath. 'Oh my. Who do we have here?'

A little girl in the front row squealed, 'There's a monster. There's a monster.'

'Good lord, what is that?' a man asked loudly from the middle of the hall.

The father with the dragon tattoo leapt to his feet and said, 'Quick, get a cage before it bites someone and they turn into an alien too. I've read about those creatures. It's dangerous for sure.'

Several of the parents charged forward. One of them grabbed a blanket from a toddler who was sitting with his mother. The little boy began to wail.

From the back of the hall, Aunt Violet caught sight of the commotion and gasped. Clementine did too. Lavender grunted.

'Pharaoh! My baby!' Aunt Violet exclaimed. 'How on earth did you get here?' The old woman rushed down the centre of the hall, sending children scattering this way and that. She elbowed the men who were racing towards the stage.

'Get away from him,' Aunt Violet roared. 'Do not lay a hand on my baby or I'll …'

'Ah!' yelled one of the men as he caught sight of Aunt Violet's angry face. She was far more petrifying than the creature on the stage.

A little girl began to cry. 'Mummy,' she sobbed, 'there's a witch.'

'No, that's just Aunt Violet. She always looks like that,' Clementine called in her great-aunt's defence.

Aunt Violet reached the stage and pushed her way to the middle, where she scooped the cat into her arms. He looked at her and hissed.

'What are you all looking at?' she challenged the audience, who were now staring wide-eyed at the terrifying woman and her equally terrifying pet.

'What *is* that?' a lady called from the back row.

'He's a sphynx, you ridiculous woman. Everyone knows that,' Aunt Violet hissed.

The audience members looked at one another and shrugged.

'He's lovely. You just have to get to know him, that's all,' Clementine announced.

'He's ugly, did you say?' a man shouted.

As always, Queen Georgiana knew just how to break the tension.

'I see we have a last-minute entrant,' she said, nodding at Aunt Violet and then turning to face the audience, who laughed loudly.

Digby Pertwhistle leaned over to Lady Clarissa and whispered in her ear. 'It looks like she'll finally get her wish.'

Clarissa nodded, although she was feeling a little sorry for Aunt Violet.

'To meet the Queen,' Digby said.

'Oh,' Clarissa nodded.

'I wonder how Pharaoh got here,' Clementine said to Poppy and Sophie, who were sitting either side of her.

'I don't know, but your Aunt Violet doesn't look very happy,' Sophie replied.

'Aunt Violet never looks very happy,' Clementine said.

Aunt Violet stood on the stage, staring at the audience and wondering what they were giggling about. The cat hissed at her again.

Aunt Violet sneered and hissed back at him. The audience hooted with laughter and so did Queen Georgiana.

In her light grey suit and oversized sunglasses, Aunt Violet bore more than a passing resemblance to Pharaoh.

'I think we have our winner,' Her Majesty declared. She took the blue rosette from the tray Mrs Marmalade was carrying behind her. 'Excuse me, dear, do you know that lady's name?' Queen Georgiana whispered to Miss Critchley, who shook her head.

'But we're not ...' Violet began to protest. 'You couldn't possibly think ...'

'And the winner of the Pet Most Like its Owner goes to –' Queen Georgiana turned towards Aunt Violet and looked at the cat. 'Well, what's his name?'

Violet gulped. 'Pharaoh,' she whispered.

'And the winner is Pharaoh and his owner,' Queen Georgiana announced. The audience went wild.

ESCAPE ARTIST

'That was fun.' Clementine beamed at her mother and Uncle Digby as they ate their morning tea outside. 'I'm so proud of Lavender and Pharaoh and Aunt Violet too.'

Her great-aunt did not feel the same way at all. She had been standing behind a tree, quietly nibbling a piece of Pierre's delicious chocolate cake and doing her best to stay out of sight. But she'd been cornered by Father Bob, who'd come to collect Adrian, his dribbly bulldog. He was congratulating her loudly on the win with

Pharaoh, who was now safely locked away in a spare cat cage that Miss Critchley had found. Violet was protesting that it was all just a ridiculous mistake. Father Bob didn't agree. He thought it was well deserved.

'Who would have thought Aunt Violet and Pharaoh would be such a hit?' said Digby. He winked at Clementine.

'Do you think we could invite Queen Georgiana to tea?' Clementine asked. 'I like her a lot.'

'Yes, the woman has impeccable judgement,' Digby grinned.

'I'm not sure that Aunt Violet would want that,' Lady Clarissa replied. She glanced towards the cake table, where something caught her eye. 'No, Pharaoh!' she shouted and ran towards him.

Aunt Violet and Father Bob looked up.

Hiding behind a huge layered sponge in the middle of the table was Pharaoh. His tail flicked from side to side like a windscreen wiper as he licked the cream from between the cakes.

Mrs Bottomley had been telling Astrid's

parents what a clever little tick their daughter was, when she heard the commotion too.

She looked up, wondering if she was seeing things.

'Why, you!' Mrs Bottomley erupted. 'I spent hours making that cake, you ugly brute.' She raced towards the table and lunged at the cat. Pharaoh darted away and Mrs Bottomley landed sprawled out, face down in the middle of the sponge.

Clementine's eyes were like saucers as she watched her teacher lying on the table with her little brown legs kicking in the air.

Aunt Violet threw her paper plate on the ground. Pharaoh raced in her direction. She quickly snatched him up but the evidence was all over his face.

Mrs Bottomley rocked backward until her feet hit the ground and she slid off the table and onto her bottom. Large chunks of cake fell from her chest as she scrambled to her feet and sped towards Aunt Violet, who was clutching Pharaoh under her arm.

'You, you horrid little beast!' Mrs Bottomley pointed her finger at the cat. Although the teacher was trembling like a jelly, Clementine marvelled that her helmet of brown curls barely moved.

'Someone must have let him out,' stammered Aunt Violet. She was looking in the direction of Pharaoh's cage and wondering which of those ghastly children had done it. Angus Archibald was standing beside the cage with Joshua, giggling behind his hands. 'It was you,' Aunt Violet hissed as she stalked towards the two boys.

Angus pulled a face. 'Was not.'

'We didn't do anything,' Joshua said and started to laugh. He was looking at the bits of pink icing stuck to Mrs Bottomley's face.

'My grandson would never do any such thing,' said Mrs Bottomley. She marched over to Aunt Violet. 'I'm sure it was … Clementine and her naughty little friends!'

Clementine frowned. She'd been standing beside Uncle Digby and her mother the whole time and Poppy and Sophie weren't even there.

Unfortunately for Mrs Bottomley, Angus had reached down to the ground just moments before and picked up the pin from the latch on the cage. He was still holding it in his hand. She saw it with her own eyes.

'Oh!' Mrs Bottomley gasped. Her bottom lip began to tremble. 'Angus Archibald!' she roared, and then started to cry.

'But I didn't do anything.' Angus shook his head and then looked at the evidence in his hand. 'It wasn't me. I just found this on the ground.'

Aunt Violet spun around and glared at the teacher. 'Ha! If I were you, madam, I would be a little more careful about accusing my great-niece in future, especially when your grandson is quite clearly the troublemaker. And what on earth are you wearing? Perhaps no one has ever been kind enough to say so, but brown is definitely not your colour!'

'How dare you?' Ethel Bottomley poked her tongue out at Aunt Violet and scurried away. Lady Clarissa raced after her. She couldn't believe what Aunt Violet had said, even if they might all have been thinking it. Angus and Joshua were wide eyed – at least for a second, until Aunt Violet got stuck into the pair of them. Once she had finished yelling, they both made a hasty exit, wiping their eyes as they went.

Aunt Violet let out an enormous sigh. As far as she was concerned the day couldn't possibly get any worse. But she hadn't noticed Queen Georgiana walking towards her.

'Oh my goodness, dear, if I didn't think you looked alike before, you certainly do now,' the Queen said with a grin.

'I don't know what you mean, Ma'am.' Violet gulped and clutched Pharaoh closer to her chest.

Queen Georgiana touched the corner of her own lip with her forefinger.

Violet wondered what she was doing.

Clementine rushed over with Lavender in tow. She pointed at Aunt Violet's face and passed her a tissue.

'What? What's the matter now?' Violet asked.

'Your lip, dear. It's covered in cream,' Queen Georgiana smiled. 'Just like that naughty little fiend.' She pointed at Pharaoh.

'Oh. Thank you,' Violet mumbled and wiped her face.

Queen Georgiana was ushered away by her bodyguard and lady-in-waiting.

'Would you like to go home, Aunt Violet?' Clementine asked. 'Lavender's exhausted. And Pharaoh looks as if he could do with a nap too.'

'Yes, I'm going right now,' Aunt Violet fumed and began to stride away.

'Can I come with you?' Clementine called. 'Mummy and Uncle Digby are staying to help clean up and I thought we could read some more of that story.'

But Aunt Violet was in no mood to babysit. 'No. I'm taking Pharaoh and you're not coming.'

Clementine frowned. Uncle Digby had disappeared inside and Sophie and Poppy were nowhere to be seen either. Her mother was near the entrance to the hall, still trying to calm Mrs Bottomley.

Clemmie hadn't noticed Angus Archibald skulking around behind her.

'You – love – a – pig,' Angus sniffled.

'Go away, Angus,' Clementine replied. 'You've made enough trouble.' She spun around to face the lad. It was obvious he'd been crying. She almost felt sorry for him.

'I didn't do it,' Angus protested. 'I didn't.'

Clementine wondered if maybe he was telling the truth. He had been a lot better the past few days.

'Where's your dog?' Clementine asked.

'Mum took him and I have to stay here and help clean up,' Angus explained between sniffs. 'Then I have to go to Nan's and she's really mad.'

'Well, you shouldn't have let Pharaoh out,' Clementine admonished. 'Aunt Violet is really cross with you too.'

'But I told you. I didn't,' Angus huffed. 'I found that pin on the ground.'

The boy stared at Lavender, who was munching on some cake that Mrs Bottomley had scraped from her chest at the height of the drama. The little pig looked up at the boy.

'Can I pat her?' Angus asked Clementine.

'Yes, but you have to promise to be gentle,' Clemmie replied.

The lad knelt down and gave the little pig a scratch behind her ear. She pressed her snout against his other hand and gave him a nibble.

Angus giggled. 'That tickles.'

'See, she's really lovely,' Clementine said. 'And she likes you.'

Angus didn't notice the shadow looming over them, blocking out the sun. When finally he glanced up, his face crumpled and he raced off to put a safe distance between him and Clementine's terrifying great-aunt.

'Well, are you coming or not?' Aunt Violet had deposited Pharaoh into the car and returned to the scene of the crime.

The child smiled up at her. 'Oh, yes please,' Clementine said. 'You take Lavender and I'll just find Mummy and Uncle Digby and let them know I'm going with you.' She thrust the pig into Aunt Violet's arms.

The old woman flinched. She held Lavender out in front of her and the little pig kicked her legs about. Aunt Violet walked back to the car, where she placed Lavender on the back seat beside Pharaoh, who was locked up in his borrowed cage.

A minute later Clementine appeared. 'I'm ready.' She hopped into the passenger seat and closed the door. 'Mummy said that she and Uncle Digby will be home soon.'

Aunt Violet started the car. 'I'm not reading anything until I've had a strong cup of tea and a lie down,' she announced.

'But you didn't say you wouldn't read to me at all,' Clementine smiled.

Aunt Violet said nothing. She simply put the car into gear and pulled away from the kerb.

Clementine turned her head to look at the animals in the back. She was surprised to see Pharaoh curled up on the seat beside Lavender.

'Aunt Violet, did you lock Pharaoh in the cage?' the child asked.

'Of course I did.' The woman kept her eyes firmly on the road ahead. 'I latched it myself.'

'Well, it's just … I think you might have to apologise to Angus,' Clementine began.

'I'll do no such thing,' Aunt Violet retorted.

'I think you should,' Clementine insisted.

'Why?' Aunt Violet snapped.

'Because Pharaoh's a magician,' the child said, frowning. If she didn't know better, she would have sworn that Pharaoh was smiling.

CAST OF CHARACTERS

The Appleby household

Clementine Rose Appleby	Five-year-old daughter of Lady Clarissa
Lavender	Clemmie's teacup pig
Lady Clarissa Appleby	Clementine's mother and the owner of Penberthy House
Digby Pertwhistle	Butler at Penberthy House
Aunt Violet Appleby	Clementine's grandfather's sister

| Pharaoh | Aunt Violet's beloved sphynx |

Friends and village folk

Margaret Mogg	Owner of the Penberthy Floss village shop
Father Bob	Village minister
Adrian	Father Bob's dribbly bulldog
Pierre Rousseau	Owner of Pierre's Patisserie in Highton Mill
Odette Rousseau	Wife of Pierre and mother of Jules and Sophie
Jules Rousseau	Seven-year-old brother of Sophie
Sophie Rousseau	Clementine's best friend – also five years old
Mintie	Sophie's white kitten
Poppy Bauer	Clementine's friend who lives on the farm at Highton Hall
Jasper Bauer	Poppy's older brother
Lily Bauer	Poppy and Jasper's mother

School staff and students

Miss Arabella Critchley	Head teacher at Ellery Prep
Mrs Ethel Bottomley	Teacher at Ellery Prep
Quentin Pickles	Caretaker
Mrs Winky	Dinner lady
Angus Archibald	Naughty kindergarten boy
Joshua	Friend of Angus's
Astrid	Clever kindergarten girl

Others

Dr Everingham	Clementine's family doctor
Daisy Rumble	Doctor's temp receptionist

CLEMENTINE ROSE
and the Perfect Present

Jacqueline Harvey

RANDOM HOUSE AUSTRALIA

For Ian, who is with me every step of the way,
and for Chris and Kimberley and Anne,
who work so hard to bring it all together

THE
INVITATION

Clementine Rose stood on her tippy-toes with her arms around her mother's waist. The woman leaned down and kissed the top of the child's golden head.

'Have a wonderful day,' Lady Clarissa said to her daughter.

'I will.' Clemmie let go and ran to the basket near the stove where Lavender, her teacup pig, and Pharaoh, Aunt Violet's sphynx cat, were snuggled together. She knelt down and pressed her face between them. Pharaoh's sandpaper tongue shot out and licked Clementine's cheek.

'That tickles, Pharaoh,' she giggled.

Lavender grunted, then closed her eyes and went back to sleep.

'Run along, Clemmie. You don't want to keep Uncle Digby waiting,' her mother instructed, then turned and headed up the back stairs. She was on her way to check that all of the bedrooms were made up, ready for the full house they were expecting on the weekend. It would be the first time since Lady Clarissa had opened Penberthy House to paying guests that every single room was booked.

Clementine wriggled into her coat and threw her backpack on her shoulders. 'Bye Mummy.' She sped towards the entrance hall.

She glanced up at the portraits of her grandparents on the wall as she flung open the front door. 'Bye Granny and Grandpa.'

Clementine hadn't noticed Aunt Violet standing on the third-floor landing.

'Does she really think you could care less,

Edmund?' the woman said as she peered at the painting of her brother. She didn't hear Lady Clarissa approach.

'Who are you talking to, Aunt Violet?' asked the younger woman.

'No one!' Aunt Violet snapped. 'You must be hearing things, Clarissa.'

Her niece grinned. 'Has Clementine got you talking to the relatives too?'

'Oh, don't be ridiculous. The child clearly lives in fairyland,' Aunt Violet said with a huff. 'I was not talking to my brother or anyone else, for that matter.'

'Well, there's no harm in it, I'm sure,' Clarissa replied. 'Clementine seems to get on rather well with all of them.'

'What a load of tripe.' Violet harrumphed and strode off towards the bathroom.

Meanwhile, Clementine Rose had met Uncle Digby and clambered into the car. The pair chatted away as they always did on the short run from Penberthy Floss to the school in Highton Mill.

The little car sputtered down the lane, which was lined on both sides by low stone walls. They soon stopped outside Ellery Prep's ornate gates and pretty hedge. Clementine leaned through the gap in the seats and kissed Uncle Digby's cheek.

He turned and grinned at her. 'Have a good day, Clemmie.'

'I will.' She hopped out of the car and ran to join Sophie, who had just arrived too.

Uncle Digby rolled down the top of his window. 'Good morning, Pierre.' His warm breath fogged up the cold glass as he called to Sophie's father, whose van was idling on the other side of the road.

'Good morning, Monsieur Digby. Please tell Lady Clarissa that the cake is almost finished and it looks beautiful.' He squeezed his forefinger and thumb together and kissed them.

'Good job, Pierre. I might pop around to the shop and have a quick look.' Uncle Digby winked. 'Just so I can put her mind at ease and let her know that it's perfect.'

'Ah, I think the cream buns will be ready too,' Pierre replied. 'I have some deliveries to make but Odette is there.'

Digby waved goodbye and eased the little car onto the road. He could have walked the short distance to the shop but the wind was chilly and he hadn't been feeling quite himself the past couple of days. He didn't want to get sick before the weekend. Lady Clarissa would have too many guests to manage without his help.

Clementine and Sophie bounded across the playground and straight to the classroom to drop off their bags. Poppy was already there talking with Astrid, the cleverest girl in the class. If anyone could be relied upon to know the answer to a difficult question it was her.

The girls greeted one another and decided to play hopscotch before the bell.

'Are you going to Angus's party?' Poppy asked the group as she threw a cold stone onto the asphalt.

Sophie and Astrid nodded. Clementine's

tummy twinged and she wondered what they were talking about.

'I don't really want to but Mummy says that it's unkind not to go, especially since he wrote the invitation himself and even put it in the mail,' Sophie explained. 'What about you, Clementine?'

'I didn't get invited,' she replied, frowning.

'Maybe the postman is running late at your house. My invitation only came yesterday,' Astrid offered.

Clementine nodded. That seemed reasonable enough. They didn't have the mail delivered every day. Her mother or Uncle Digby had to go to Mrs Mogg's store to collect it.

Angus and Joshua raced past the girls.

'You'd better get me good presents,' Angus called. 'Otherwise I'll tie you up and feed you to the dragon.'

'Yeah, you'd better,' Joshua yelled. 'His dragon is really mean.'

Clementine wrinkled her nose. 'I bet his dragon is bossy too, just like him and his nan.'

Sophie looked at Clementine and coughed loudly.

Mrs Bottomley was standing right behind the group. 'What was that, young lady?'

The child spun around.

'Nothing, Mrs Bottomley,' Clementine lied. As the teacher also happened to be Angus's nan, Clementine hoped she hadn't heard her.

'I'll have you know that my daughter is going to a lot of trouble for this party. Even though I told her it was a ridiculous idea to have it after school, when the children will be tired and grumpy. I've been asked to make the cake, which I trust will not be eaten by some ghastly cat this time.' Mrs Bottomley was referring to the last sponge cake she'd made, which had been nibbled by Aunt Violet's cat, Pharaoh, at the pet day and then completely ruined when Mrs Bottomley fell into it. 'I suggested that she leave some of the students who might not be able to behave themselves properly off the guest list.'

Mrs Bottomley arched her eyebrow at Clementine and walked away.

Clementine felt another twinge in her tummy. What if she really wasn't invited? Did Mrs Bottomley think she couldn't be trusted at a birthday party? That wasn't true at all. There were plenty of other kids in the class who were naughty – Joshua, for a start. He was always in trouble, especially with Miss Critchley, the head teacher.

Sophie pulled a face. 'She's so mean.'

'Don't worry, Clementine. If you're not invited I'll tell Mummy I don't want to go either,' Poppy said.

'I don't want to go to Angus's stupid party anyway,' Clementine declared.

But that wasn't true at all. By morning tea time Clementine had learned that the whole class had been invited. Every – single – one. Except her. There was even a dress-up theme: kings and queens, princes and princesses. Angus said that he was only having the queens and princesses so that the kings and princes could capture them and feed them to the dragon that lived in the cave at the bottom of his garden. Astrid said that was rubbish because everyone knew dragons weren't real. Clementine wasn't so sure but she hoped Astrid was right.

Clementine loved to dress up. She even had the perfect outfit, which Mrs Mogg had made for Clemmie's own princess party the year before. It was a pink gown with lace, and a hooped skirt underneath to make it stick out, just like a proper princess dress. She had a silver tiara with pink stones in it and her mother had found a long pearl necklace and a pearl bracelet in one of the trunks in the attic. Deep down, Clementine hoped that when she got home that afternoon, the invitation had arrived.

LEFT OUT

'Angus is having a party, Mummy,' Clementine told her mother when Lady Clarissa picked her up from school.

'That's nice, Clemmie,' her mother replied distantly. She was mentally checking off some of the jobs she still had to get done before the weekend.

'Everyone's invited –' Clementine began.

'That's very kind of Mr and Mrs Archibald.'

'– except me,' Clementine finished sulkily.

'Oh dear, that's no good,' said Lady Clarissa. She glanced between the road and Clemmie's crestfallen reflection in the rear-vision mirror.

'Were there any letters today?' Clemmie asked hopefully.

'Not that I remember, darling. But we can check when we get home. When's the party?'

'After school on Tuesday. But I don't care.' Clementine wiped a hand across her eye. 'Angus is horrible.'

'I thought you were getting on better with him,' her mother said calmly.

Clementine shrugged. 'Mrs Bottomley said that she told Angus's mum not to invite any troublemakers and then she looked straight at *me*.'

'Never mind, Clemmie. I could phone Angus's mother and see if there's been a mistake, if you like,' Lady Clarissa suggested.

'No! Then he'll just say that I'm a crybaby. I don't want to go.'

'If that's how you really feel, I'm happy not to interfere. There's so much to do at home and I certainly need your help this weekend.' Lady Clarissa smiled in the rear-vision mirror. 'Poor Uncle Digby is run off his feet and Aunt Violet's being her usual unhelpful self.'

Clementine decided not to think about Angus and his party again. There were much more interesting things going on at home.

When her mother first told her there was to be a wedding at the house, Clementine had been bursting with excitement. She couldn't stop talking about it. She'd never been to a wedding before.

'But where will everyone sit?' Clementine had asked her mother at the time. Penberthy House was big but the dining room could fit only twenty people at the most.

'We're going to put a tent in the back garden,' her mother had explained.

'A tent? But that's even smaller than the dining room.' Clementine wondered if the people getting married were tiny, like pixies or elves.

'Oh no, Clemmie, this tent will be enormous,' her mother had reassured her.

'Like the circus?' Clementine had asked. Her mother and Uncle Digby had taken Clemmie to the circus the last time it came to the showground at Highton Mill.

'A little bit like that,' her mother had replied.

'But without the elephants or the lions,' Clementine decided.

It had all seemed so far away when her mother first mentioned it. It was before Aunt Violet had come to stay and before Clemmie had started school. And now there was only one more day until the men would come and put up the tent and then the guests would begin to arrive. Every room had been booked by the wedding party and their families.

Lady Clarissa turned into the driveway and Clementine spotted Mrs Mogg's car parked next to Uncle Digby's.

'Oh, that's a relief,' Lady Clarissa exhaled. 'Margaret said she'd pop over and help Uncle Digby with some of the cleaning this afternoon.'

Clementine thought she could ask Mrs Mogg if she'd brought any letters too. She didn't *really* care about Angus and his party, of course. But she'd check anyway, just to be sure.

A BIG TENT
FOR A BIG DAY

On Saturday morning, Clementine Rose sat on the back steps of the house. She was watching the men hammering a line of long metal spikes into the ground. A large sheet of canvas was spread across the lawn like a giant white blanket. She couldn't wait to see it transform into the tent. Lavender was sitting beside her, dozing in the wintry sun. Both girl and pig were wearing matching pretty blue jumpers, which Mrs Mogg had knitted a few weeks earlier.

Friday at school had been awful. Everyone had been talking about their costumes for Angus's party and Angus had demanded all sorts of presents. Clementine's invitation had never arrived, so she decided that she would just ignore the other kids and think about what was happening at home.

But a sick feeling returned to the bottom of her tummy whenever anyone mentioned it. Even Angus had asked her about his present. She definitely wasn't getting him anything if she wasn't invited.

The weather had turned much colder in the past few days, and with the last autumn leaves scattered across the ground, Clementine thought the garden looked a bit sad and scruffy. She wondered if the tent would be warm enough, but her mother had assured her that this wouldn't be any ordinary construction. Clementine thought it was looking a lot bigger than the little triangle in which she and Sophie played in Sophie's backyard.

Digby Pertwhistle emerged from the house

and stood on the step beside Clementine and Lavender. 'Hello there, you two.'

Clementine looked up and smiled. 'Hello Uncle Digby. Do you think the tent will be finished soon?'

The old man frowned. 'I hope so. There's still a lot to do. At least when the marquee is up, there'll be one less thing for your mother to worry about.'

'What's a marquee?' Clementine asked.

'It's just a fancy name for the tent, Clemmie,' Uncle Digby replied. 'I don't think brides like the idea of having their weddings in a common old canvas tent.'

Clementine felt an excited shiver run through her whole body. She couldn't wait to see the bride in her dress.

'It's a big job,' Clementine declared.

'Yes, it certainly is,' Uncle Digby said. He could recall only one other wedding at the house. It was when a very young and beautiful Violet Appleby had married her first husband. Sadly, the fellow left her and took a lot of her money with him a couple of years later. At the time Uncle Digby was just a young man, and had only started working as the family butler a year before.

'Can Lavender and I help with anything?' Clementine asked.

'Mmm.' Uncle Digby tapped his forefinger against his lip. Most of the remaining jobs involved polishing and cleaning, and letting Clementine loose with a feather duster was not the best idea. Last time she'd helped she had accidentally knocked over one of the family's heirloom vases, chipping the top.

'I've got an idea,' said Uncle Digby. 'Why don't you practise one of your poems and then perhaps you can entertain the guests when they arrive later?'

Clementine nodded. 'I've got that new one you taught me. I could tell it to Mr Bruno and his men. They must get a little bit bored hammering pegs into the ground.'

Uncle Digby smiled at Clementine. 'Just don't get in the way.'

'I won't.' She stood and walked down the steps. 'Come on, Lavender.'

The little pig opened her eyes and scrambled to her feet.

Clementine marched into the garden and climbed onto a bench ready to begin her recital.

One of the older gentlemen working nearby had learned the exact same poem when he was a lad, and soon enough he was saying it along with her.

'You're a clever girl. What's your name?' the man asked when she had finished and taken a bow.

'Clementine,' she replied.

The man grinned at Clemmie. 'Have you got another one for us?'

Clementine loved nothing more than an audience. She knew several poems by heart; her favourite was by a man called Mr Dahl and it was about an anteater. All of the men listened this time. Above the clanking of their hammers, all that could be heard was

Clementine and the odd grunt of approval from Lavender.

Upstairs in the house, Aunt Violet was fiddling with some knick-knacks on her dressing table, when she heard Clementine's voice outside. She wondered what the child could possibly be up to.

The old woman peered through the window. She was horrified to see Clementine nattering at the workmen who'd been stomping about the garden since yesterday afternoon.

Aunt Violet pushed the window up further and poked her head outside. 'Clementine, what are you doing? Those men are here to work, not to listen to your gobbledegook.'

'Oh, hello Aunt Violet,' Clementine called back. 'I'm just practising.'

'You should find somewhere else to do it,' Aunt Violet said. 'Those men don't have time to stand about.'

'But I've no one else to practise with,' said Clementine. She thought of the portraits in the entrance hall. 'Except for Granny and

Grandpa, and they don't laugh as much as these men do.'

'Your grandfather didn't laugh much when he was alive, Clementine. I can't imagine the old trout has changed a jot since he's been dead,' Aunt Violet sneered.

A stout young man looked up at the window. 'It's all right, ma'am. She's not in the way and she's very funny.'

'Clementine, come away from those people at once,' her great-aunt demanded.

'What people?' the young fellow said suspiciously. 'Aren't we good enough to listen to some poetry?'

'I don't know what you mean,' Aunt Violet fumed. 'But I'll be reporting your bad manners to whoever is in charge.'

'That's Mr Bruno.' Clementine pointed at the short fellow in front of her. 'He's the boss.'

Mr Bruno looked up at Aunt Violet's scowling face and then back at Clementine. 'Is she always so lovely?' he asked the girl.

Aunt Violet grumbled something under her breath and then slammed the window so hard that the panes rattled.

'Oh no, she's not lovely at all,' Clementine replied. 'She's Aunt Violet.'

MAGIC

By midday, Mr Bruno and his men had finished their tightening of ropes and hammering of pegs, and in the middle of the back lawn stood an enormous white tent. Clementine thought it looked like a giant wedding cake. Another group of people had arrived and set up lots of round tables, and stacks of chairs were being wheeled into place too.

Clementine and Lavender were having a wonderful time exploring inside, when into the marquee blew the most extraordinary man Clementine had ever seen.

'Oh my, oh my, there's no time, no time, we must get to work. Places everyone, we need to get this show on the road,' he burbled. 'Chop, chop!'

Clementine and Lavender watched from underneath a table. The man wore a bright blue suit, a red bow tie and matching red shoes. A red-and-yellow spotted handkerchief poked out of his blazer pocket. He flapped his hands about as if he were directing traffic at a busy intersection. A stream of people poured into the tent behind him, carrying all manner of things, from huge floral arrangements to rolls of shimmering fabric.

Clemmie's eyes were like dinner plates as she took it all in.

The man clapped his hands together. 'It's not much now, but just you wait and see. Places everyone, let the magic begin.'

Clementine wondered if he was going to put on a show. She scrambled out from under the table and jumped up in front of him.

The man leapt into the air. 'Good gracious, my dear. Where did you come from?'

'Hello,' said Clementine, 'I like your shoes.'

The man peered over the top of his stylish spectacles. 'Oh, thank you. Who do we have here?' His brow furrowed as he caught sight of Lavender, who trotted out and sat beside her mistress.

'I'm Clementine and this is Lavender,' Clemmie replied.

'How darling.' The man surveyed the child in her pretty ensemble and the pig in its matching jumper. He bent down to scratch the top of Lavender's head. She leaned into his fingers and squirmed with delight. 'Aren't you the cutest little piggy in the world? And I just adore your matching outfits.'

'Mrs Mogg made them for us,' Clementine explained. 'Are you a magician?'

A row of lines puckered the man's forehead.

'You said, "Let the magic begin",' Clementine reminded him.

'Yes, yes, I suppose I am a magician of sorts.

Just give me a couple of hours and this tent will go from drab to fab. This wedding is going to be perfect with some magic from Sebastian. That's me, of course. Sebastian Smote at your service.' He rolled his hand and made a bow.

Clementine giggled. 'You're funny.'

'I am here to entertain,' Sebastian replied. 'But dear little girl and dear little piggy, might I suggest that you pop outside to play? When you return, you will not recognise this place, I assure you.'

Clementine would rather have stayed put and watched the magic happen, but she could hear her mother calling her.

Lady Clarissa poked her head inside the entrance. 'I thought you'd be here, Clemmie. Come along and let Mr Smote do his work. It's time for lunch.'

'Goodbye,' Clementine said with a wave. 'I can't wait to see what your magic looks like.'

The man grinned at her, and then hurried away to direct the delivery of an enormous chandelier.

'No, no, no!' he called as there was a loud crash.

'I love weddings,' Clementine enthused as she and her mother walked back to the house, with Lavender a few steps behind. 'Even though I've never been to one before.'

'I just hope it goes smoothly,' said Lady Clarissa. She smiled tensely at her daughter. She'd had at least ten calls that morning from the bride's mother, a pushy woman called Roberta Fox. The last call was about the colour of the soap in the bathrooms. Lady Clarissa had been wondering if she'd made the right decision about having the wedding.

There was also the small challenge of Aunt Violet, who could always be relied upon to upset someone. Lady Clarissa had employed half the village to help with the arrangements and Mr Smote was in charge of making sure it all came together, so with any luck Aunt Violet would stay right out of the way. If it all went well, Lady Clarissa hoped she'd be able to pay for a new roof for Penberthy House without selling the Appleby family jewels after all.

'When will the guests come?' Clemmie asked.

'Everyone's due to arrive this evening,' her mother replied. 'I know you're looking forward to it, Clemmie, but you must remember that *we're* not guests. You can look from a distance but please don't get in the way.'

Clementine nodded. 'I just want to help. And see the bride, of course.'

'Yes, I know you do. It's very important that we get this right. A wedding is one of the biggest events in anyone's life and I want to make sure that the bride and groom have only happy memories of their special day at Penberthy House,' her mother explained.

'Well, you'd better keep Aunt Violet out of the way because she doesn't make anyone very happy,' Clementine said seriously.

'I think she's been trying harder, don't you?' her mother asked, raising her eyebrows.

'Maybe.' Clemmie shrugged. 'I like when she

reads to me. But she was cross about Pharaoh sleeping in my room with Lavender. I told her that she could take Lavender's basket and borrow them for the night and then she said "ick" and pulled a cranky face. But I think she's only pretending. I saw her giving Lavender a scratch the other morning, but when I asked what she was doing she said Lavender was being a nuisance and she was shooing her downstairs.'

Lady Clarissa stifled a grin. 'Never mind, Clemmie. Now, I have lots of jobs to finish this afternoon. Let's get some lunch and then perhaps you can play in your room for a while.'

Lavender grunted as if to agree.

'Okay,' Clemmie replied and squeezed her mother's hand.

AUNT VIOLET

C lementine climbed onto a chair opposite her great-aunt at the kitchen table.

'Hello Aunt Violet.'

'Hmph.' The woman didn't look up from the newspaper she was reading.

'Are you excited?' Clementine asked.

Aunt Violet ignored the child completely and kept on reading.

Clementine pinched her forefingers and thumbs together and held them in the air.

'Aren't you just a l-i-i-i-i-ttle bit excited, Aunt Violet?'

Violet Appleby sighed. She folded the newspaper in half and placed it on the table. 'And what exactly should I be excited about? The fact that we're about to be overrun by people I don't care to meet or that there's rain forecast for tomorrow? Mmm?'

Clementine frowned at her great-aunt. 'The wedding. I'm so excited about the wedding and seeing the bride in her beautiful dress. I'm not sure which dress I'll wear tomorrow. I can't decide between my favourite red one and the yellow one Mrs Mogg made me for Christmas last year.'

'Clarissa, the child does realise that she's not *invited* to this ghastly occasion, doesn't she?' Aunt Violet looked at her niece, who was standing at the bench cutting Clementine's cheese sandwich into triangles.

'Of course, Aunt Violet. Clemmie's just excited. We've never had a wedding at the house before and you have to admit, it's always lovely to see a bride on her special day.' Clarissa arranged Clemmie's lunch on a plate and set it down in front of her.

'I can't think of anything worse,' Aunt Violet said with a sneer.

Digby Pertwhistle had been listening to the conversation while he filled the kettle at the sink. He turned and looked at Aunt Violet. 'That's strange, Miss Appleby.'

'Why do you say that?' she asked.

'I thought you must love weddings. Haven't you had four of them?'

'Four!' Clementine looked at her great-aunt. 'Have you been a bride four times?'

'Frankly, that's none of your business,' snapped Aunt Violet. 'And I'll thank you not to bring up the subject ever again, Pertwhistle.'

'You must have been beautiful, Aunt Violet,' Clementine said. 'Especially if you looked like the lady in the painting on the stairs.'

Aunt Violet sniffed. 'Yes, well, I suppose I was rather an attractive young woman.'

'Can you tell me about your dresses?'

Clementine asked. 'Did you wear a white gown?'

'Several, I should think,' Uncle Digby muttered under his breath. Lady Clarissa nudged him.

'Clementine, we are not talking about it. Eat your lunch,' Aunt Violet ordered.

Clementine reluctantly turned her attention to the sandwich on her plate. After a couple of bites she looked up and saw that Aunt Violet was staring at her.

'Would you like some?' Clementine held out a triangle.

'Heavens no. I'll have my own, thank you. That's if anyone could be bothered making me one.'

'What would you like, Aunt Violet?' Clarissa asked.

'Ham and a hint of mustard and some tomato and cheese. Oh, and some of that lovely egg mayonnaise that you make so well.'

'It won't be long,' Clarissa sighed. Her patience for Aunt Violet and her demands was wearing thin, particularly as Clarissa had so many things to do before the guests arrived. 'Aunt Violet?'

'Yes.'

'Digby and I have a lot of jobs to finish this afternoon. Would you mind popping down to Mrs Mogg's and getting a few things for me? And I haven't collected the mail from yesterday, either.'

'I'll come too. We can take Lavender for a walk. She loves going to the village,' Clementine added.

'I don't think so. I'm awfully tired. I was planning to have a rest this afternoon,' Aunt Violet replied bluntly.

'It's all right, Clarissa. I'll go.' Digby patted the young woman on the arm. He hadn't been feeling one hundred per cent himself, but it didn't seem fair for Lady Clarissa to have to run this errand.

'You've got more to do than I have,' Lady Clarissa protested. 'Really, Aunt Violet, we've all got to pitch in.'

'You don't have to use that tone with me, Clarissa,' Aunt Violet barked. She pressed her palm to her forehead. 'I can feel one of my headaches coming on.'

The old woman stood up.

'Where are you going, Aunt Violet?' Clementine asked.

'To my room. Not that it's any of your business.' She walked towards the back stairs. 'You can bring my lunch up when it's ready, Clarissa. And I'd like some tea too. Come, Pharaoh.'

Aunt Violet's sphynx cat had been sleeping in the basket in front of the fire. He arched his back and meowed loudly, before padding over to where Lavender was sitting. He began to lick the side of the little pig's face.

'Urgh. I said come.' Aunt Violet glared at the cat, which ignored her completely. 'Have it your way, then. I think you've been infected by that ghastly pig.'

She stomped upstairs and out of sight.

'Lavender's not ghastly,' Clementine whispered as she disappeared. 'You are!'

Her mother and Uncle Digby remained silent, but they were both thinking exactly the same thing.

AN OUTING

After lunch, Digby Pertwhistle met Clementine and Lavender at the back door. A chill wind had sprung up and Clementine had put on her favourite pink coat and long snuggly boots with lamb's wool lining.

Uncle Digby grabbed his scarf and coat from the rack beside the door and the trio set off for the village, armed with Lady Clarissa's list.

'Don't forget the mail,' she called after them.

The garden was quiet but inside the marquee

was a hive of activity, with Mr Smote and his assistants in the midst of their decorating. Two large stone lions now guarded the entrance to the tent.

'Look at those!' Clementine gasped. 'How did they get there?'

Uncle Digby pointed to a little tabletop truck with a crane on the back. 'I think that's how.'

'People go to a lot of trouble for weddings, don't they?' Clementine marvelled as she hung back, trying to get another glimpse inside the marquee.

'Come along, Clemmie, we'd best hurry up. I still have some polishing to finish when we get back.' The old man lengthened his stride and Clemmie and Lavender ran to catch up.

Even though she'd almost put Angus's party completely out of her mind, Clementine couldn't help wondering if there might be some mail for her at the store.

By the time they crossed the stream and passed the church to arrive at Mrs Mogg's store, Uncle Digby was completely out of breath.

'Are you all right?' Clementine asked as he sat down heavily on the bench outside.

'Yes, yes, just a bit tired. Must be old age catching up with me.' He smiled reassuringly at Clementine as she tied Lavender's lead to one of the chair legs.

Uncle Digby pushed open the door and the little bell tinkled. Clementine skipped in ahead of him to the toasty warmth of the shop. Today it smelt like hot pies and cinnamon. The old man pulled Lady Clarissa's shopping list from his coat pocket while Clementine went straight to the counter.

Margaret Mogg walked through from the flat that was attached to the back of the building.

'Hello there, Clementine,' she greeted the child warmly. 'And what can I do for you today?'

'Hello Mrs Mogg. Uncle Digby has a list and Mummy asked if I could collect the mail,' Clementine said importantly.

'Of course.' Mrs Mogg turned to the pigeonholes behind the counter. Everyone in the village had their own little cubbyhole for the mail, as there was no postman in Penberthy Floss. 'Well, that's odd.' She peered into the empty space. 'Nothing here at all, Clementine.'

Clemmie frowned. She didn't want to think about Angus's stupid party any more. She wasn't going and that was that.

Mrs Mogg thought it was very unusual. In fact, she couldn't remember a day when there'd been no mail for Lady Clarissa. The woman was always winning competitions and seemed to get an awful lot of bills too.

Mrs Mogg walked back to the counter and looked over at Clementine. 'How are things coming along at the house?'

'Very well, thank you. The marquee is up. That's a fancy name for the tent,' Clementine explained. 'And Mr Smote is decorating it inside and he's even put two giant lions at the entrance to stand guard.'

Mrs Mogg gasped and put her hand to her mouth. 'Lions?'

'Oh, they're not real. They're made of stone. Uncle Digby said that it's probably got something to do with the man who's getting married. He's from another country, and they have lions on their flag,' Clementine explained.

'Ah yes, your mother said that he was Sri Lankan, so that makes sense. I wonder if the bride will wear a white gown or a sari,' Mrs Mogg said.

'What's that?' Clementine asked.

'Saris are beautiful, Clemmie. They're sort of like a wraparound dress but far more complicated and with thousands of sparkles on the fabric,' said Mrs Mogg.

'Can you make one for me?' Clementine asked.

'I don't think so, dear. They're very specialised.'

Clementine was disappointed. She liked the idea of a dress with thousands of sparkles on it.

The doorbell tinkled and Clementine was surprised to see Joshua from school and his mother.

'Good afternoon, Mrs Tribble,' the shopkeeper called.

'Oh hello, Mrs Mogg,' the woman replied. Joshua raced to the counter, his eyes scanning the lolly jars, which contained all manner of treats. He didn't even notice Clementine standing beside him.

His mother reached the counter too. 'I was wondering if you had any cardboard. I have to make his royal highness here a crown for Tuesday.' Mrs Tribble glanced at her son, who was attempting to lift the lid on the container of red frogs.

'It's for Angus's party,' Joshua said. 'I'm going to be a king.'

Clementine felt as if she'd been slugged in the tummy. She decided to go and find Uncle Digby before Joshua noticed her.

'Are you going too, Clementine?' Mrs Mogg asked.

Clemmie quickly shook her head.

'Oh, that's a pity. It must be for the boys,' the old woman said.

'No. It's for girls too. Everyone's going.' Joshua looked at Clementine, and then poked out his tongue at her.

He didn't realise that his mother was watching. She placed her hand firmly on his shoulder. 'Joshua Tribble, last time I looked you were a boy, not a lizard. Apologise at once.'

This time Joshua's mouth stayed closed.

His mother tightened her grip.

'Ow!' Joshua complained. 'You're hurting me.'

The woman leaned down and whispered something into his ear.

'Sorry,' he spat.

'I didn't hear you,' Mrs Tribble said through gritted teeth.

Joshua folded his arms and said with a scowl, 'Sorry, Clementine.'

Clementine said nothing.

Mrs Mogg rubbed her hands together. 'Ahem. Right then. The cardboard is just over in the school supplies.'

'Thank you, Mrs Mogg.' Mrs Tribble grabbed Joshua's hand and headed for the middle of the shop.

'But you said I could have a lolly,' the boy whined.

Clementine couldn't hear exactly what Mrs Tribble said but she thought it sounded like she was going to give him something else.

'Why don't you have a look at some of the lovely new fabrics that came in last week, Clementine?' Mrs Mogg suggested with a smile.

Clementine nodded. Her tummy still didn't feel right, but she walked to the far corner of the shop, where Mrs Mogg kept all of the material, buttons and threads.

Everyone in the village knew about Clemmie's sense of style. Her mother didn't know where it came from, given that the child had arrived in a basket of dinner rolls and been adopted by Lady Clarissa. Clementine and Mrs Mogg shared a love of pretty things. The elderly woman had made Clementine lots of dresses and other bits and pieces over the years. Mr and Mrs Mogg had never had any children, so Clementine was the closest thing they had to a granddaughter and they adored her.

'How are you getting on back there, Digby?'

Mrs Mogg called. 'Is there anything I can help you with?'

Mrs Mogg's shop was always pleasantly heated but today Digby Pertwhistle felt as if he'd walked into a blast furnace. Tiny beads of perspiration formed on his temples and he hastily wiped them away with the back of his hand.

'Yes, thank you, Margaret,' he called back. 'Would you mind locating me some lemon-coloured soap?'

A few minutes later, with Mrs Mogg's help, Uncle Digby had managed to find everything on Clarissa's list and was now standing at the counter packing them into his grocery bag.

'Are you all right, Digby?' Mrs Mogg noticed that his face had turned a rather horrible shade of grey and he seemed to be sweating.

'Yes, it's just a bit warm in here.' He removed his scarf and used it to mop his brow.

'Well, take care of yourself. The last thing Lady Clarissa needs is you getting sick. And tell her I'll be there first thing in the morning to help. Clyde can look after this place for the day.' She was referring to her husband, who preferred watching television to serving in the shop.

Clementine heard Uncle Digby and Mrs Mogg talking and hurried back to them.

'Did you see anything you liked, Clemmie?' the old woman asked.

Clementine shrugged.

'Are you sad about that party?' Mrs Mogg whispered as she leaned forward on the counter.

'A little bit,' Clementine replied.

'Never mind, sweetheart. We can't all go to everything. And no one else is having a wedding at their home this weekend, are they?'

Clementine smiled. 'No, that's true. And I do like the red material with the spots.'

'Ah, that's my girl. I thought you might like that one. Goodbye dear.' Mrs Mogg turned to Uncle Digby. 'And take care of yourself.'

The old man nodded. 'See you tomorrow, Margaret.'

EMERGENCY

Clementine, Lavender and Digby Pertwhistle walked up the front driveway just as a black station wagon reversed into one of the parking spaces.

'Looks like some of the guests have arrived early,' Uncle Digby said with a worried look. He had struggled to keep up with Clementine and Lavender on the way home and was feeling far worse than earlier. He was cross with himself for getting sick, and today of all days.

Clementine ran ahead and greeted the

dark-haired man who hopped out of the car. 'Hello. Are you here for the wedding?'

'Yes. My brother's the groom. Are you here for the wedding too?' he asked, wondering if the child was a friend of the bride's family.

'No, I live here with Mummy and Uncle Digby and Lavender.' She motioned towards the pig, which was snuffling about beside her.

'Oh, you're a lucky girl then,' the man replied.

'Except when it rains,' Clementine said.

The man looked at her curiously. 'I don't quite follow.'

Clementine remembered that her mother had told her to stop telling the guests about the leaking roof so she changed the subject. 'It doesn't matter. Are you on your own?'

'No, my wife and children are upstairs getting settled. They'll be thrilled to meet you. And you –' He bent down to give Lavender a scratch. 'I don't think the children have ever seen a pet pig before.'

'She's a teacup,' Clementine said. 'Well, she's a lot bigger than that now.'

'Hello there.' Uncle Digby puffed as he caught up. 'Welcome to Penberthy House. I'm Digby Pertwhistle.'

Just as Uncle Digby said his name, he let out a gasp of air and collapsed to the ground, scattering the groceries all over the place.

'Uncle Digby!' Clementine shouted.

The guest swung into action. 'Run and tell your mother to phone for an ambulance.'

Clementine's face crumpled.

'Don't worry. I'm a doctor.' He smiled at her kindly and then turned his attention to Uncle Digby, who looked as if he was asleep.

Clementine raced up the front steps and into the house. 'Mummy, Mummy,' she called as she ran into the kitchen. Her mother was stirring something on the stove.

Lady Clarissa turned around. 'What is it, Clemmie?'

Clementine's words spilled out in a panicky rush. 'It's Uncle Digby. He's fallen down outside and the man said you need to get an ambulance.' Her mother raced to the telephone and dialled the emergency number. She gave the house's name and address and ran to the front door.

Digby Pertwhistle didn't remember falling over. But now when he tried to lift his head, the whole world seemed to be spinning.

'Mr Pertwhistle you need to lie still,' the man beside him instructed.

'What happened?' Digby asked, holding his hand to his head.

'I'm not sure but we must get you to the hospital for a check-up.'

'No, I can't possibly leave now. There's far too much to do.' Uncle Digby's chest tightened and the words came out as a wheeze.

'Oh, thank heavens,' Lady Clarissa exclaimed as she reached the pair and saw that Uncle Digby was conscious. 'Is he all right, Dr Gunalingam?'

The man was looking at his watch and taking Uncle Digby's pulse. 'Well, he's awake, but I'm not prepared to take any chances. Is the ambulance on its way?'

'Yes, it will be here soon.'

'Is Uncle Digby going to be okay?' Clementine asked.

'Yes, darling, I'm sure he'll be just fine. Can you run upstairs and ask Aunt Violet to come down? Someone needs to go with Uncle Digby to the hospital. And take Lavender inside too,' Lady Clarissa instructed.

In the distance, a siren began to wail.

Clementine called the little pig, who came racing to the front door with her lead bumping along the ground behind her. Clementine ran up the main stairs to the third floor. She barged straight into the Blue Room.

'Aunt Violet,' she said, puffing.

'Haven't you heard of knocking? It's not new, you know.'

Clementine ran back to the door and rapped on it sharply.

'What now?' the old woman grumbled. 'Can't you see I was reading?'

'It's Uncle Digby. He fell down outside and the ambulance is coming,' Clemmie blurted. 'Mummy wants you to go to the hospital with him.'

'Well, why didn't you say so?'

Clementine was confused. She did say so.

Aunt Violet sprang into action. She stood up, smoothed her trousers and shoved her feet into her leopard-print ballet flats. Clementine had never seen her great-aunt move so quickly.

'Come on then, what are you waiting for?' the old woman asked Clementine. 'An invitation?'

Together they rushed down the stairs and out the door. At the front of the house, they saw Uncle Digby lying on the ground, covered by a throw rug that Clarissa had retrieved from the sitting room.

'What's the matter with him?' Aunt Violet demanded. She stared at Digby, whose eyes were wide open and staring back up at her. 'I thought you were dying.'

'Sorry to disappoint you, Miss Appleby.'

'Well, are you sick? Or did you just fall over?' she asked tightly.

Clarissa took her aunt by the arm and guided her away from Uncle Digby and the doctor.

'Dr Gunalingam thinks Uncle Digby might

have something wrong with his heart,' Lady Clarissa whispered. 'I don't want to frighten Clementine but one of us has to go to the hospital with him.'

Aunt Violet pursed her lips. 'Don't look at me. I'm not having Pertwhistle die on my watch.'

'I don't think that will happen but if you're not prepared to go then you'll have to stay here and greet the guests. There are quite a few groups about to arrive,' Clarissa explained.

Aunt Violet was about to tell Lady Clarissa that she couldn't possibly be left in charge when the ambulance roared into the driveway with the lights flashing and siren blaring.

Clementine was sitting beside Uncle Digby holding his hand.

The old man managed a weak smile. 'Don't look so worried, Clemmie. I'll be fine.'

'But I don't want you to go, Uncle Digby.' Tears spilled onto her cheeks.

He squeezed Clemmie's hand. 'Darling girl, it's just a check-up. I'll be back before you've had time to miss me. I can't leave your mother and Aunt Violet with all of the wedding preparations now, can I?'

Clementine shook her head. 'No. Aunt Violet makes Mummy too stressed.'

'Yes, I think you're right about that,' the old man agreed.

The paramedics soon had Uncle Digby on a stretcher and ready to go into the back of the ambulance. Lady Clarissa turned to her aunt. 'Aunt Violet, the bride and her family will be arriving soon. And the groom and his parents too. This lovely man here, who has been so kind and helpful, is Dr Gunalingam, the groom's brother.'

The doctor looked up from where he was monitoring Uncle Digby and nodded at Aunt Violet.

'His wife and their three children are upstairs already. You'll have to arrange some afternoon tea for them, please. Pierre delivered some cakes just a little while ago.' Lady Clarissa ignored Aunt Violet's protests and hugged Clementine,

then climbed into the back of the ambulance. 'Oh, and the room allocations are on the kitchen sideboard. Please make sure that everyone gets the room they're supposed to have.'

The doctor climbed into the back of the ambulance next to Lady Clarissa. 'Please tell my wife where I am,' he called out to Clementine and Aunt Violet.

The driver closed the back doors and ran around to the cabin.

'But, but,' Aunt Violet was aghast. 'Clarissa, you can't leave me in charge. I don't know anything about being hospitable.'

Clementine gave her great-aunt a puzzled look. 'You're not going to the hospital.'

'I said hospitable, Clementine. It means . . . Never mind. I don't know the first thing about how to run this place.'

'Don't worry, Aunt Violet. Lavender and I will help you.' Clementine smiled up at her great-aunt, who seemed to have steam coming out of her ears.

ARRIVALS

After the ambulance left, Clementine and Aunt Violet walked back inside. Her great-aunt began to ascend the stairs.

'Where are you going?' Clementine asked.

'Back to my book,' Violet replied.

'But Mummy said that we need to tell the doctor's wife where her husband is and then make some tea,' she reminded her.

'Godfathers,' Aunt Violet muttered under

her breath and thumped back downstairs. She followed Clementine to the kitchen.

'I can't put the kettle on, but I can help with the cakes,' said Clementine. She noticed a large sponge cake sitting on the sideboard and some of Pierre's chocolate-chip biscuits beside them. She retrieved a little pile of plates from the dresser and put them around the scrubbed pine table.

'They're not taking tea out here,' Aunt Violet protested.

Clementine stopped and thought for a moment. 'I can take everything to the dining room, if you'd like.'

Aunt Violet considered the effort required to move to the other room. 'No, I'm sure the woman and her children will understand, given that we're short-staffed. Set it up out here.'

Clementine carefully placed the cake and the biscuits in the middle of the table.

'You might as well run upstairs and fetch them,' Aunt Violet said reluctantly. She took the kettle off the stovetop and poured the water into the large teapot.

Clementine bounded up the back stairs. She wasn't sure which room the family was in but the Jasmine Suite at the end of the first floor corridor seemed likely. It had two adjoining rooms and Lady Clarissa had recently installed some bunk beds she'd won in a competition. The suite was now perfect for a family staying together.

Clementine knocked on the door. She was greeted by a pretty woman with long dark hair and a very large tummy.

'Hello. My name is Clementine and I live here. Mummy asked me to tell you that your husband has gone to the hospital with Uncle Digby and Mummy, and Aunt Violet and I have made some tea for you and your children,' she explained.

'Oh,' the lady replied. 'I wondered where he'd got to. We heard the siren but couldn't see what was going on. Is everything all right?'

'Uncle Digby fell down. They're just going

to the hospital to check everything's okay,' Clementine explained.

The sound of giggling came from the adjoining room. Clementine craned her neck to see who was making the noise.

'That's the children,' the lady said. 'They've never slept in bunk beds before so they're a little excited. Arya, Alisha, Aksara, come and meet Clementine,' she commanded.

Three children with the most beautiful sparkling brown eyes poked their heads around the doorway and waved.

Clementine giggled as they appeared – one, two, three.

The girls made a dash and hid behind their mother's skirt but the little boy stayed in the doorway.

'They're not really shy.' The woman leaned around and looked at them.

'Would you like to come downstairs?' Clementine asked. 'We have chocolate-chip biscuits and a sponge cake that Uncle Pierre made and he's the best baker in the world.'

At the mention of food the girls skipped out and said hello. The little boy ran over to join them. Clementine led the group down the back stairs and into the kitchen where Aunt Violet was cutting the cake.

'Hello there. I'm Karthika,' the mother introduced herself. 'And this is Arya, who's five, and Alisha, who's three. And Aksara – he's two. This little one is Asha and she'll be here soon.' Karthika patted her belly. 'It's a pleasure to meet you.'

The old woman looked up and glared at the family. 'Yes, I suppose it is.'

'That's Aunt Violet,' Clementine chimed in.

Aunt Violet cut a huge slice of sponge and dumped it roughly onto one of the plates. Clementine wondered why Aunt Violet had to be so cranky. Fortunately, the group was distracted by the front doorbell ringing.

'I'll get it,' Clementine volunteered, but she didn't move.

'Go on, then. I've got my hands full,' Aunt Violet told Clementine. 'And there'd better be nothing wrong with that silly old fool Pertwhistle,' she muttered under her breath. 'I don't know how we'd ever manage without him.'

AUNT VIOLET MEETS HER MATCH

Clementine opened the front door. Three people stood in a huddle on the steps. There was a couple, who looked older than her mother, but younger than Uncle Digby, and a very pretty young woman.

'Hello,' said Clementine.

'We're here for the wedding,' said the man with a look of surprise. He wondered why they were being met by a child.

'My name is Clementine. Please come in,' said Clemmie. She was trying to remember exactly what her mother usually said when she greeted the guests.

The trio walked into the hallway but the lady turned around just as Clemmie was about to close the door. 'Uncle Orville,' she called in a singsong voice. 'Uncle Orville? Where are you?'

'Hector,' the woman said sharply, as she turned and looked at her husband. 'Go and find your uncle. Now!'

Clementine jumped. So did the young woman and Hector. He scurried off outside to locate the missing member of their party.

The woman smiled like a shark at Clementine. 'Where is your mother?'

'Mummy and Uncle Digby have gone to the hospital with the doctor. He's the groom's brother and it was lucky he was here when Uncle Digby fell down. I'm looking after everyone with Aunt Violet,' Clementine explained.

'Oh, I'm sorry to hear that,' said the young woman. 'My name's Harriet Fox.'

'Oh!' Clementine gasped. 'You're the bride. Mummy told me your name.'

The woman beamed. 'Yes, that's right.'

'I can't wait to see your dress. And the tent is going to be so beautiful –' Clementine prattled.

The older woman cut them off. 'Yes, yes, of course she'll be beautiful, she's my daughter. And I should hope we have a marquee and not a tent. Now, if you'll go and fetch your aunt, I'd rather like to get settled in our rooms. We've had a long drive.'

The young woman rolled her eyes at her mother and then smiled secretly at Clementine.

'Okay.' Clementine marched off towards the kitchen. Uncle Digby had been right about brides being funny about marquees. Well, bride's mothers.

Meanwhile, Aunt Violet was studying the room allocation list and trying to work out what it all meant. She had a red pen in hand and seemed to be doing some allocating of her own.

'Aunt Violet,' Clementine called. 'The Foxes are here.' Then she giggled. 'I hope the chickens are locked away.'

'What? What chickens? What are you talking about?' Aunt Violet asked the child disdainfully.

Mrs Gunalingam laughed and so did Arya. The woman winked. 'We got it.'

Violet Appleby strode out of the kitchen towards the entrance hall.

'I'd better go too,' said Clementine reluctantly. 'Aunt Violet's not always the most helpful with the guests.'

Mrs Gunalingam nodded. After a few minutes alone with the woman she knew exactly what Clementine was talking about.

Clementine caught up to her great-aunt in the hallway.

'Violet Appleby,' said Aunt Violet as she looked at the mother and daughter. She didn't feel the need for any additional niceties.

'It's lovely to meet you, Miss Appleby.' Harriet Fox extended her hand, which Aunt Violet ignored completely.

'Your rooms are on the second floor. Let me see –' Aunt Violet scanned the list, which was attached to a plastic clipboard. 'Mr and Mrs Fox are in the Peony Suite and Harriet, you're in the Rose Room.'

'What about Uncle Orville? Roberta asked.

Aunt Violet ran her finger down the list. 'He's not here.' She tapped the pen she was holding on the page.

'What do you mean he's not here?' Roberta Fox fumed. 'Of course he's here.' She went to snatch the clipboard from Aunt Violet's hand.

Aunt Violet clutched it to her chest.

'Give me that!' Roberta tugged at the board.

Aunt Violet made a fierce face at her. 'No!'

'Your niece said that she could accommodate the whole family and Uncle Orville is part of the family so I want to see where she has put him.'

Aunt Violet clung to the clipboard.

'Oh look,' Roberta Fox peered over Aunt Violet's shoulder. 'There's Uncle Orville with your father now.'

Aunt Violet turned and just as she did, Roberta Fox tore the clipboard out of her hands.

'Why, you!' Aunt Violet's mouth gaped open.

Roberta scanned the list. 'I think you've been doing some creative rearranging, Miss Appleby. Just wait until your niece gets wind of this.'

'It's my house and I can put people wherever I jolly well want,' Aunt Violet huffed.

Roberta Fox wrinkled her nose like an angry otter. 'Why don't you go and make a fresh pot of tea? This little one can help us find our rooms.'

'I can do that,' Clementine agreed.

Aunt Violet stormed towards the kitchen.

The front door opened and Mr Fox appeared at last with Uncle Orville in tow. The old man wore a smart suit with a waistcoat and a bowler hat. Clementine thought he looked as if his face could do with an iron – there were so many crinkles.

'It says here that Uncle Orville is in the Daffodil Room,' said Mrs Fox.

Clementine gasped. 'But that's my room.' She wondered when her mother had planned to tell her about that.

'All right then, shall we go?' asked Hector Fox. He looked at Clementine, who was suddenly feeling a lot less excited about the wedding party.

Clementine led the group upstairs. First she showed Harriet to the Rose Room, which she seemed to like very much. The Peony Suite was a little further along the corridor. Then she had to take Uncle Orville up to her room. She was surprised when she opened the door to find that most of her things had gone and even her wardrobe was bare. It can't have been a mistake. Her mother had clearly planned to give her room away.

'I hope you like it,' Clementine said grumpily. She looked around for Lavender's basket and even that was missing. 'Stupid wedding,' she said under her breath.

'Thank you, dear,' the old man said. He smiled sweetly at her. 'It's a very nice room.'

'Yes, I know,' she snapped. 'That's because it's mine.'

'No, no, dear, I don't need anything else.

I'll be fine.' The man nodded and put his tiny suitcase on the bed to unpack.

Clementine walked out of the room and down the hallway. She knew she shouldn't be cross about having to give up her room but she wished that her mother had warned her. And why couldn't Aunt Violet have given up her room instead? Clemmie stopped at her mother's bedroom door. She turned the handle and peered inside. Her schoolbag, her doll's house and all her toys were piled in the corner. She opened the wardrobe. Her mother had hung all of Clementine's clothes inside and Lavender's basket was at the bottom. A mattress was made up at the foot of her mother's bed. And in the corner she noticed a large suitcase.

Downstairs, the doorbell rang again. As Clementine scurried downstairs, a terrible thought came to her. She hadn't seen Pharaoh or Lavender for a long time. Her mother would be very unhappy if they'd been locked in one of the guest rooms.

Clementine opened the front door. A

handsome young man was standing on the step. 'Hello,' he said. 'I'm Ryan. The groom.'

'Hello.' Clementine held the clipboard in front of her. She felt very official and important. 'Do you want to check which room you're in?' she asked. 'I can't read much yet. I'm only five.'

The man took the page and had a quick look.

'Here it is. I'm in the Blue Room.'

'The Blue Room?' Clementine said nervously. 'But that's Aunt Violet's room.'

'Sorry? Do you think there's been a mistake?' he asked.

Clementine shook her head. 'No. I'll show you where it is.' She marched upstairs feeling quite pleased. If it was good enough for her to give up her room, then it was good enough for Aunt Violet too.

It wasn't long before the groom's parents arrived, completing the wedding party staying at the house. Clementine helped them to their rooms without any assistance from Aunt Violet, who was still making tea.

Clementine invited everyone to the kitchen – not that Mrs Fox was impressed at all.

Everyone seemed to know each other, which Aunt Violet found a blessed relief. She hated making small talk. Clemmie was pleased to see that Pharaoh and Lavender had emerged from their hiding place and were now playing a vigorous game of chasings with the three children.

'Clementine, why don't you take the children and Lavender for a walk in the garden,' Aunt Violet said testily.

'Oh, I'm not sure about that,' said Karthika anxiously. 'It's getting cold outside.'

'It was *not* a suggestion,' said Aunt Violet.

'Let's go and get your coats, shall we?' Karthika instructed.

The telephone rang and Clemmie ran to pick it up. 'Hello, Penberthy House,' she said, just as her mother had taught her. 'Oh, hello Mummy. Is Uncle Digby all right?'

Her mother could hear the hubbub in the background. 'What's happening there, Clemmie?' she asked.

'Afternoon tea,' the girl replied.

'In the kitchen?' her mother asked.

'Yes, Aunt Violet said that it was a pain to have it in the dining room or the sitting room.'

'Oh, good gracious!' Lady Clarissa fussed. 'These people are paying very good money to stay at the house. I'm sure they didn't expect tea in the kitchen.'

'No, Mrs Fox was very cross,' Clemmie informed her mother quietly, as she didn't want the woman to hear her.

'Did everyone find their rooms?' Clarissa asked.

'Yes,' Clemmie replied.

'Clemmie, I'm sorry about moving you. There was a last-minute change of plans and I didn't have time to tell you or Aunt Violet. Is she very upset?'

'I don't know, but she and Mrs Fox had a fight,' Clemmie explained.

Lady Clarissa groaned. 'I'll be back as soon as I can. Can you ask Aunt Violet to put the legs of lamb in the oven, please? She'll need to peel the potatoes too – they're on the sink. Mrs Mogg will be there in a little while – I called and asked her to help with the dinner.'

'Is Uncle Digby all right?' Clemmie asked her mother again.

'We're not sure,' her mother said truthfully. 'But he's being very well looked after.'

Clementine suddenly felt sick herself. She didn't care about having to share her room with her mother or even Aunt Violet. She just wanted Uncle Digby to be better and back at home where he belonged.

WEDDING EVE

Clementine hung up the telephone and quietly informed Aunt Violet what her mother needed done. Aunt Violet couldn't believe that she was going to have to prepare the evening meal too. This was far too much. She immediately set about clearing the afternoon tea.

'But I haven't finished,' Roberta Fox said in astonishment. She clung to her teacup as Aunt Violet picked up the woman's plate, which still contained a large chunk of cake.

'Perhaps you should eat a little more quickly, Mrs Fox,' Aunt Violet said. 'Some of us have work to do.'

'If you'd served the tea in the sitting room, you wouldn't have this problem now, Miss Appleby.' Roberta tugged the plate from Aunt Violet's grip and set it down with a thud.

Aunt Violet narrowed her eyes. She wasn't about to admit that the woman was probably right.

'Run along, Clementine,' Aunt Violet instructed. 'Take those little ones outside.'

It was the last thing Clementine felt like doing but she decided it was better not to argue with Aunt Violet. She took her coat from the peg by the back door, pulled on her boots and ushered the three children out into the garden. Lavender followed hot on their heels.

'She's lovely,' Alisha said to Clementine as she bent down to give the piggy a scratch.

'Yes, she is,' Clementine agreed. But she couldn't bring herself to smile. She was too worried about Uncle Digby. And lurking in the back of her mind was the unpleasant memory of seeing Joshua at Mrs Mogg's shop. He'd seemed so pleased about Angus's birthday party.

'Are you sad?' Arya asked.

Clementine nodded. 'Uncle Digby never gets sick.' She didn't want to say that she was upset about Angus's stupid party too.

'Don't worry. Our daddy is an expert at broken hearts. I'm sure he can fix your uncle,' Arya told Clementine seriously. She reached out to hold Clementine's hand.

Clementine took it. 'Really?' she asked.

'It's true,' Arya said, smiling now. 'Mummy said that he went to school *forever* to learn how to do it.'

Clementine felt a little bit better already. 'Would you like to see the garden?'

A chorus of 'yes' went up. It was good to have something to take her mind off Uncle Digby and the hospital, Clementine decided.

'Let's see if Mr Smote has finished his decorations inside the marquee,' Clementine said. 'That's just a fancy name for the tent,' she told the younger two, who nodded their heads up and down.

Aksara ran ahead but jumped back when he saw the lions guarding the entrance. His eyes were huge.

'It's all right,' Clementine reassured the little boy. 'They're not real.' She pulled back the heavy fabric that had been hung across the doorway. He tiptoed past the lions.

Clementine gasped as she took in the decorations. 'Mr Smote *is* a magician.'

The ceiling was draped with the most beautiful shimmering silver fabric and a giant crystal chandelier hung from the centre. The chairs looked like presents, wrapped up with bows on their backs, and the tables were laid with shiny silverware and white plates with silver trim.

Clementine spied the magician himself on the far side of the marquee, and walked towards him. 'Hello Mr Smote.'

'Hello there, Clementine. What do you

think?' He held his arms out with a flourish.

'It's beautiful,' Clemmie sighed.

'And the flowers aren't even here yet.' He rubbed his hands together. 'Just wait until you see it tomorrow morning.'

'Mummy says I can only poke my head in. I'm not going to the wedding, but my friends are.' She motioned at the children who were standing beside her. 'It's their uncle who's getting married.'

'Well, I do hope that you enjoy yourselves,' Mr Smote said. 'And what do you think of my lions?'

Aksara looked up at him with wide eyes. 'Big.'

The girls giggled.

'Yes, they are, aren't they? I've heard that the groom loves them,' said Mr Smote.

Arya nodded. 'Our daddy's his brother and he does too.'

'Well, you'd better be running along. I have to get home to paint a castle,' said Mr Smote.

'A castle?' Clementine gasped. Penberthy

House was big enough. She couldn't imagine what it would be like to live in a castle.

'How do you paint a castle?' Arya asked.

Mr Smote looked at the children's stunned faces. 'Oh no, I'm not painting a real castle. My godson is having a birthday party next week and I offered to create a miniature castle for the party.'

Clementine couldn't believe her ears. She wondered if Mr Smote was *Angus's* godfather. If he was in charge of the party then it would be incredible for sure. She wished even harder now that she could go.

'All right, I'm about to lock up for the night,' Mr Smote said as he walked towards the entrance.

Clementine was curious about how he could do that. Tents didn't have proper doors, after all.

'You don't need to lock up,' Arya said.

'Why not?' Mr Smote asked

'Because there are lions on guard,' she said with a smile.

Mr Smote laughed. 'Yes, you're right about that.'

'And a pig too,' Clementine added. Lavender was sitting right in the middle of the two stone beasts.

'She's a guard pig,' Alisha giggled. Lavender grunted as if to agree.

The children headed back inside just before dark. Clementine had decided the best thing she could do was forget all about Angus and his party and concentrate on the wedding and playing with her three new friends.

Mrs Gunalingam met them at the back door and guided her children straight upstairs to their baths.

Inside, Margaret Mogg was stirring the gravy on the stove. Clementine stood on tiptoe to watch. 'I'm glad you're here, Mrs Mogg.'

'We couldn't let the guests starve, could we?' said Mrs Mogg. She left the wooden spoon in the saucepan and opened the oven to check on the lamb.

Clementine's nostrils twitched. 'It smells delicious. Is Mummy home yet?'

'She telephoned a little while ago. Aunt Violet is driving over to pick her and the doctor up,' Mrs Mogg explained.

'That's a relief,' said Clementine.

The sound of the front door opening distracted the pair and Clementine ran off into the hallway.

'Mummy!' Clementine launched herself at her mother's waist. From out of nowhere, tears sprang from her eyes and she began to cry in big shuddery sobs.

'Oh Clemmie, sweetheart, what is it?' Her mother knelt down and Clementine clung to her like a periwinkle in a rock pool.

'I – don't – know,' she gulped.

'Clemmie, Uncle Digby will be fine. Please don't worry. He wouldn't want to see you like this.'

Lady Clarissa brushed a rogue strand of hair

from Clementine's wet face. 'I know it's been a difficult day, what with all the excitement of the wedding and then the worry about Uncle Digby. But I'm sure that tomorrow will be much brighter.'

Clementine didn't tell her that she'd been upset about seeing Joshua and hearing Mr Smote talk about a party too, or that she was mad about having to give up her room, or that Aunt Violet had been even crosser than usual. She didn't want to sound like a crybaby.

'Come along, Clemmie. Let's go and wash your face and then we can get ready for dinner. Mrs Mogg has been busy – something smells delicious.'

Lady Clarissa stood up. Clementine grabbed her hand and the two of them walked to the downstairs bathroom where Clementine splashed some water on her face and dried her eyes.

'Where's Aunt Violet?' Clementine asked between sniffs.

'She went straight upstairs to move her

things into Uncle Digby's room for the night. I had to tell her in the car that I'd given her room away too and she'd be bunking in with us. But now, of course, with Uncle Digby away, she's decided to take his room. She wasn't nearly as cross as I expected but I think that was because Dr Gunalingam was in the car too. No doubt I'll hear about it later when everyone's gone home.'

Clementine nodded. Her mother was right about that.

No one noticed the little pile of mail on the hall table. Just as Aunt Violet had been about to leave to pick up Lady Clarissa and the doctor, Father Bob had turned up on the doorstep clutching a bundle of letters that had been among his mail. He'd been very surprised to find them, as Mrs Mogg never made mistakes with the post. Then again, she had left Mr Mogg in charge on Thursday afternoon when she'd been helping at Penberthy House and Clyde wasn't known for his attention to detail.

NIGHT
TERRORS

L ady Clarissa glanced at the kitchen clock. It was already past midnight and she had just finished the washing up and sent Margaret Mogg on her way. Fortunately, dinner had gone well and the guests seemed to be enjoying themselves. She thought that the bride and groom seemed very well suited, although Roberta Fox had certainly not been any less demanding in person. Clarissa had been glad when Aunt Violet skulked off to bed early complaining of another imaginary ailment. Her aunt had done enough damage that day and Clarissa thought she couldn't possibly upset anyone from her bed.

In the eerie quiet, Lady Clarissa wondered if Uncle Digby was all right. She missed him terribly; over the years she'd come to rely on him as much as she would have her own father. A tear spilled onto her cheek and she brushed it away. She couldn't bear the thought of anything happening to him. She shook the notion from her head. Of course he'd be fine – there wasn't any other option.

Meanwhile upstairs, Aunt Violet awoke wishing she hadn't had that last cup of tea before bed. She peered into the darkness. After a few moments she remembered that she had been banished to Pertwhistle's bedroom, which at least had a bathroom attached. In fact, it wasn't a bad room at all. Perhaps she'd swap. She tottered off to the toilet, not bothering to put on the light.

Further down the hallway, Orville Fox felt the same urge. He put on his dressing-gown and slippers and headed along the corridor to the bathroom. A few minutes later, he shuffled back to his room and opened the door, stubbing his toe and wondering who had put the wooden trunk near the bed in the time he'd been out.

Orville sat down, took off his slippers and eased out of his gown. He adjusted the pillows and rolled onto his side and within just a few seconds he was fast asleep.

Lady Clarissa finished drying the last saucepan. From somewhere high in the house, a bloodcurdling scream shook the windows. She leapt into the air, threw the saucepan onto the bench with a clatter and ran up the back stairs two at a time.

Clementine woke with a start. She sprang out of bed and ran along the corridor towards Uncle Digby's room. There was an awful noise coming from inside. When she opened the door and flicked on the light, her eyes almost popped out of her head.

'Aunt Violet, what's going on?' she gasped.

Lady Clarissa ran into the room behind her.

Violet Appleby was standing beside the bed, her face as white as a sheet and her hair standing on end as if she'd poked her finger into a power point. Her breathing was shallow and she looked as if she was trying to speak.

'Mummy, there's a man in Aunt Violet's bed!' Clementine exclaimed.

'Get him out of here!' Aunt Violet shrieked, prodding the intruder's side with her forefinger. 'Get him out of here NOW!'

But Orville Fox was sound asleep. Clearly the man could have slept through a cyclone, because he'd just met Hurricane Violet.

MIXED UP

Clementine rubbed her eyes. For a moment she had forgotten where she was. She took a few seconds to remember that she was on a mattress at the foot of her mother's four-poster bed.

She could hear the pitter-patter of raindrops against the window.

'Mummy,' Clementine called. But there was no reply. She sat up and saw that her mother's bed was already made.

Clementine threw back the covers and

shivered. Lavender and Pharaoh were curled up together in Lavender's basket near the radiator.

She grabbed her dressing-gown, stuffed her feet into her woolly slippers and headed out along the corridor to the back stairs. As she passed by her own bedroom, the door opened and she was met by Uncle Orville.

He must have stayed put after his earlier adventure. Half the house had come running after Aunt Violet's scream. In the end, Mr Fox and Dr Gunalingam had carried Uncle Orville back to Clementine's room, much to the relief of Aunt Violet. She said that she was going to barricade the door.

The man squinted at Clemmie. 'Hello dear.'

'Good morning, Mr Fox,' she said. 'Did you have a good sleep?'

'Yesh, yesh, but I had a terrible dream about a wild woman who was shcreaming like a witch . . .'

Clementine wondered why he was talking strangely.

'Are you joining ush for the wedding today?' he asked.

Clementine couldn't believe that she'd almost forgotten about it. Of course, that's why Mr Fox was dressed up. He might have been old and a little off kilter, but he was a very snappy dresser.

'I like your suit,' Clementine said, admiring the pinstripes and the lovely silk handkerchief that was poking out of his pocket. 'But you might want to change your shoes.'

Mr Fox looked down at his slippered feet.

'Oopsh.' He turned and walked back into the room. 'I wash a tailor you know.'

'Really?' Clementine was impressed. 'Mrs Mogg makes all my clothes. I think she's very clever. She can make just about anything . . . Although, I don't know if she could make a suit.' She followed him inside the room.

Clementine glanced at her bedside table and noticed what she first thought was a glass of water. Then she looked more closely.

'Mr Fox, I think you've forgotten something else too,' she said, pointing.

'Oh, thank heavensh.' Mr Fox shuffled over and reached into the glass. He popped his teeth into his mouth and gave Clementine a big smile.

Other children her age might have been frightened, but Clementine had seen plenty of false teeth at the house before. In fact, she even had a couple of sets that guests had left behind. She sometimes made up plays with the talking teeth, much to her mother's and Uncle Digby's horror.

'You look very nice, Mr Fox,' said Clementine, grinning back at him. 'Even better with your teeth.'

Clementine said goodbye and raced down the back stairs to find her mother and Mrs Mogg busily preparing breakfast. Violet Appleby was dressed and sitting at the table sipping a cup of tea.

'Oh, hello, sleepyhead.' Her mother glanced at the clock on the wall. It was half past nine.

'Half the day's gone, Clementine,' her great-aunt commented. 'Why don't you run along and get dressed. I presume you still want to see that wedding?'

'Yes, of course,' said Clementine.

The smell of bacon filled the room as Mrs Mogg opened the oven and retrieved a plate piled with crispy rashers. She trotted off to the dining room.

'Would you like something to eat first, Clemmie?' her mother asked.

The child nodded. Her stomach was making all sorts of funny gurgles.

'What about an egg and some bacon on toast?' her mother suggested.

'Yes, please.'

Lady Clarissa turned to her aunt. 'Aunt Violet, would you like to see Uncle Digby this morning? Then I'll go later tonight.'

Clementine looked up expectantly. She'd hoped Uncle Digby would be home today.

'No,' Aunt Violet said tersely. 'I'm far too tired. Some of us didn't have a good night at all.'

'But that's not Mummy's fault,' said Clementine.

'Of course it is,' Aunt Violet snapped. 'If she'd bothered to have locks installed on the bedroom doors, I'd never have been confronted by that ghastly man – who, by the way, was missing his teeth!'

Lady Clarissa changed the subject. 'Well, Aunt Violet, do you think you could manage to give Mrs Mogg a hand this morning with some tidying up? The caterers will be here soon – thankfully everything is pre-prepared and they just have to use the ovens to heat things up.'

'I'm exhausted, Clarissa,' Violet snapped. 'And you've employed half the village to help. Why do I have to get involved?'

Lady Clarissa stood firm. 'Aunt Violet, with Uncle Digby in hospital we are still short-staffed.'

'Well, it's just like him to bunk off when we're busy,' Aunt Violet complained.

Clementine had been getting crosser by the second. 'It's your fault Uncle Digby's not here!'

'I beg your pardon, young lady?' Aunt Violet turned sharply to look at the girl.

'If you hadn't made Uncle Digby go to the shop with me yesterday afternoon he'd still be all right. You made him sick!' Clementine pushed the plate of bacon and eggs so hard that the bacon scattered all over the table.

'How dare you?' Aunt Violet's lip trembled. 'I did no such thing, Clementine.' She stood up and strode towards the back stairs.

Clementine began to cry. She'd never felt so mixed up inside. One minute she was excited and the next minute she was worried about Uncle Digby or sad that she hadn't been invited to Angus's party. Clementine didn't like it at all.

Lady Clarissa rushed over and wrapped her arms around Clementine, giving her a big hug.

'I'm sorry, Mummy,' the girl sniffed. 'I didn't mean to upset Aunt Violet.'

'It's all right, darling. I know we all want Uncle Digby home as soon as possible. But really, it's not Aunt Violet's fault that Uncle Digby is sick.' Lady Clarissa kissed her daughter's cheek.

'Why don't you finish your breakfast, then run along upstairs and get dressed. I'm sure that Mrs Mogg would love to see you in one of her pretty dresses. And then you can pop out into the garden with Lavender and watch everything from there.'

Mrs Mogg smiled at Clementine, who sniffled once more and then nodded back.

AUNT VIOLET
TO THE RESCUE

Clementine did exactly as her mother suggested. She put on one of her favourite dresses, a lovely red one with a matching coat. She added her shiny red boots and finished off the ensemble with a bow in her hair and a scarf around her neck.

Clementine was on her way downstairs when a shriek filled the house. She ran down to the second floor, and was greeted on the landing by the bride's mother. Mrs Fox was wrapped in a towel and dripping water all over the floor.

'Tell your mother there's no hot water,' Roberta Fox shouted at Clementine. 'How am I supposed to get ready for the biggest day in my life when I can't even have a hot shower?'

Her husband Hector emerged, already dressed, from the bedroom.

'That's funny, dear. I thought it was the biggest day in our daughter's life,' he chided.

'You know what I mean, Hector. Just go and find someone to fix it. NOW!' she screeched.

Orville Fox was on his way downstairs when he ran into the group.

The old man winked at his niece-in-law. 'I'm afraid you might have to put on more than that for the wedding.'

His nephew chortled loudly. 'I was thinking just the same thing myself, Uncle Orville.'

'Oh, stop being ridiculous, the pair of you!' Roberta glared at her husband and his uncle, who scurried away downstairs.

Clementine was just about to suggest that

Mrs Fox could use the bathroom upstairs instead, when Aunt Violet appeared.

She pushed past the woman and straight into the bathroom. Clementine dashed after her. She was surprised to see Aunt Violet giving the taps some rather violent attention, and then banging on the old boiler in the corner.

'That's done it,' Aunt Violet announced as she ran the taps. Steam began to pour from the room.

Clementine stared at her great-aunt in amazement. 'You fixed it!'

'Of course I did.' The old woman strode back into the hallway and Clementine followed.

Roberta Fox barged into the bathroom and slammed the door.

'Don't bother thanking me.' Aunt Violet pursed her lips and hurried away down the corridor with Clementine close behind.

'But how did you do that? Mummy says that Uncle Digby is the only one who can ever fix the hot water in there,' Clementine said.

'I lived here for a long time too, Clementine,'

Aunt Violet replied. 'And that heater has been the same ever since I can remember.'

'I thought Mrs Fox was going to burst, she was so cross.' Clementine smothered a giggle as she remembered the woman's expression.

'Well, we wouldn't want that now, would we?' Violet kept her eyes straight ahead and walked towards the main stairs.

'Aunt Violet?' Clementine called.

'What is it this time?' The old woman turned and stared at Clementine. She couldn't help thinking that the child looked rather sweet in her red ensemble.

'I'm sorry about what I said before. Uncle Digby isn't sick because of you.'

The woman coughed sharply and turned away. 'Don't be so sure of that,' she mumbled, but Clementine didn't hear her.

'Do you want to go for a walk outside?' Clementine asked.

'I'll come with you in a little while,' Aunt Violet replied. 'Mrs Mogg needs some help first.'

Clementine could hardly believe her ears. She wondered if something had happened to Aunt Violet. Clemmie glanced up at the portraits on the wall. Maybe her grandpa had had a word.

THE BEST DAY EVER

Clementine ran downstairs and threw open the front door. There were cars all over the driveway and Mr Smote was barking orders as tall floral arrangements were carried through the garden towards the marquee.

'Hello Mr Smote,' Clementine shouted.

'Good morning, Clementine,' he called back.

She thought his clothes looked even smarter than the day before. 'That's a lovely tie.'

'Why, thank you, Miss Appleby,' he said and dipped into a bow.

The clock in the hall chimed and Clementine counted off the strikes. She wondered where Harriet Fox was – it couldn't be too much longer until the wedding. Her mother had said that it would start at midday and the clock had just chimed eleven times.

A white van pulled up and two men jumped out and began unloading a pile of enormous presents wrapped in silver paper with white bows.

'Oh!' Clementine gasped. 'They're so pretty.'

And that's when the idea came to her. She should find Uncle Digby a present to cheer him up. Not just any old present; this one had to be perfect, so that he'd know how much she wanted him to get well and come home.

Clementine wondered what she could get him. She didn't have very much money in her piggy bank. And the only shop close by was Mrs Mogg's, and she didn't really sell a lot of things Clemmie thought Uncle Digby would like.

Maybe she could ask her mother to take her to the village later on, once the wedding was underway. Clementine closed the door and turned around. At the top of the stairs she saw the most extraordinary sight.

'You look like a princess,' Clementine gasped, as she took in Harriet Fox's beautiful gown. It was white and covered with silver sparkles. Her long blonde hair was pulled back into a perfect bun and she was wearing a shiny tiara.

Harriet beamed. 'Thank you, Clementine. I feel like a princess today. Have you seen the children?'

Clementine shook her head.

'They're in the wedding too. Arya and Alisha are my flower girls and Aksara is the pageboy,' Harriet explained.

Clementine couldn't wait to see them all. A moment later, Mrs Gunalingam appeared on the landing behind Harriet with the three children in tow. She was wearing a beautiful purple and red wraparound dress with thousands of tiny sparkles all over it. Right behind her, the two little girls wore the prettiest white dresses, which were tied at the waist with large purple bows. Their tiny brother wore a black suit with a sparkly purple bow tie.

'You all look beautiful,' Clementine gasped. She remembered her conversation with Mrs Mogg at the shop. 'Is that a sari?'

'That's right, Clementine.' The woman spun around to show off the whole garment.

'It's so pretty,' Clemmie said.

A man carrying a huge camera skirted the group at the top of the stairs and walked halfway down. He pulled out the tripod legs and set up to take some photographs.

'We'll take some more shots inside the house before we head out into the garden,' he instructed.

He arranged the children on the stairs in front of the bride. Clementine watched, spellbound. When they finally moved into the front sitting room for some seated pictures, Mrs Gunalingam whispered something to the photographer.

'Yes, of course, ask her to join us.'

'Clementine, would you like to have a picture with Harriet and the children?' Mrs Gunalingam asked.

Clementine clapped her hands together. 'Yes, please.'

The man showed the group to their positions and then snapped away. Clementine beamed for the camera.

Mr and Mrs Fox arrived downstairs with Uncle Orville. Clementine decided that she would go and find her mother, Aunt Violet and Mrs Mogg, and let them know that the wedding was about to start. They could watch from the garden.

Lavender was snuffling about Clemmie's feet as she entered the kitchen. She clipped the little pig's red lead onto her collar. She thought she'd better not risk upsetting the guests by allowing Lavender to wander around on her own.

Outside, a large group of people had gathered in the walled garden for the ceremony. Clementine admired all of the gorgeous outfits;

there were women wearing sparkly saris like Mrs Gunalingam's and others dressed in pretty gowns. The men looked handsome too. And Mr Smote was smiling as he watched on from the side. The rain had cleared and the sun was shining.

Clementine stood between her mother and great-aunt as Harriet Fox and her father walked down the makeshift aisle behind the three dark-haired children. A string quartet played and Clementine thought it was the most beautiful music she'd ever heard.

Everyone oohed and aahed as Aksara tried to scatter rose petals from a little basket. He soon grew tired of his job and tipped the basket upside down, dumping a pile of petals onto Uncle Orville's foot. The guests roared with laughter.

During the ceremony, the bride and groom said a lot of words before exchanging rings. Then they kissed. Clementine closed her eyes. Kissing was yucky.

Afterwards, the guests moved into the marquee while the bride and groom posed for photographs with their family. Clementine loved watching the children climb up onto the lions outside the tent for a special picture.

'Well, that's that then.' Mrs Mogg smiled at Clementine. 'What did you think?'

'It was beautiful. I can't wait to be a bride. But I don't want to have to kiss a boy.' Clementine screwed up her face at the thought.

Aunt Violet raised her eyebrows. 'I think that's a long way off, young lady.'

'I should think so.' Her mother laughed and squeezed her hand.

'I don't know about you lot, but there's a warm fire and a cup of tea inside,' Mrs Mogg said. She turned to go.

'That is an excellent plan,' Aunt Violet nodded.

Clementine shivered. 'Won't they be cold out here in the tent?'

'Oh no, I had a quick peek earlier. Would you believe they have heaters in there? At least if it rains it will be drier than inside the house,' Mrs Mogg declared.

'Perhaps you should leave the tent up, Clarissa, and we can all move in there,' Aunt Violet suggested, raising her eyebrows playfully.

'You might be right about that, Aunt Violet. We'll have to move out when I can afford for the roof to be done.'

Clementine looked at her mother. 'We won't really have to live in a tent, will we, Mummy?'

'No darling, I'm sure that we can find somewhere else just for a little while,' her mother replied.

'Perhaps you should all head off on a holiday,' Mrs Mogg suggested.

'Yes please.' Clemmie clapped her hands together.

'Maybe.' Lady Clarissa slipped her hand into Clementine's and together the group headed back inside to the snuggly warmth of the kitchen.

Mrs Mogg filled the kettle and Aunt Violet went to the sideboard to find some cups and saucers. Clementine wondered if there was something wrong with her – she was being so helpful.

Her mother went to the pantry to fetch the teacake Pierre had delivered that morning along with the giant layered wedding cake.

Lavender was lying on her back and enjoying a belly scratch from Clementine.

'Oh, that reminds me, was there any mail yesterday?' Lady Clarissa asked as she set the cake on the table.

Margaret Mogg turned from where she was pouring the tea. 'No. It was very strange indeed.'

Violet Appleby coughed, then scurried from the room. When she returned, she placed a bundle of letters on the table. 'Father Bob brought these over yesterday afternoon as I was leaving to pick you up, Clarissa. He said that it was in among his. I completely forgot about it too. It's probably just bills, anyway, although you do seem to have a knack with those competitions.'

Margaret Mogg sighed deeply. 'I can't leave

that husband of mine in charge for more than a minute. I am so sorry, Clarissa. I hope there wasn't anything important.'

Clementine washed her hands and sat up at the table beside her great-aunt. She looked at the letters, trying not to get her hopes up again.

Lady Clarissa flicked through the pile. 'Bill, bill, bill. Oh!' She drew in a sharp breath and handed Clementine an envelope. 'This one's for you.'

'For me? What is it?' she asked, her eyes wide.

Clementine tore open the envelope and unfolded the card inside. There was a picture of a king and her name was beside it in large scribbly writing.

'What does it say?' she said excitedly, and showed the card to Aunt Violet.

'Wait a minute, I have to get my glasses.' The old woman picked them up from the table. 'It says, "You are invited, Clementine Rose!"'

'Yippee!' Clementine's arms shot into the air. 'He didn't leave me out on purpose.'

Her great-aunt scowled at the interruption. 'Do you want to hear the rest?'

'Yes, please.' Clementine clapped her hands together.

Aunt Violet read the details, including what time and where the party would take place.

Clementine's mouth fell open. 'Oh!'

'What's the matter now?' her great-aunt asked. 'I thought you wanted to go to the party – even though you pretended that you didn't.'

'I don't have a present. Angus said that we all had to get him something good or he'd feed us to the dragon that lives at the bottom of his garden,' Clementine said seriously.

'For heaven's sake. I wouldn't want to go to his party if he said that to me,' Aunt Violet declared. 'And you do know that there are no dragons living at the bottom of his garden, don't you? The boy has an overactive imagination.'

Clementine was not so sure. Angus could be very convincing when he wanted to be.

'Will you take me to the village later?' Clementine asked her mother. 'I have to find the perfect present for Uncle Digby too.'

Mrs Mogg poured three cups of strong black tea.

'Oh darling, I don't think I have time today. But perhaps . . .' Lady Clarissa glanced at Aunt Violet.

Clemmie followed her gaze. 'Aunt Violet, will you take me? Please?' Clementine looked up at the older woman, her blue eyes sparkling.

'I don't know, Clementine. I have some things to do . . .' Aunt Violet sipped her tea.

'Pretty please?'

Aunt Violet stared at the girl's pleading expression. 'Oh, all right,' she relented.

Lady Clarissa and Mrs Mogg exchanged smiles.

Clementine couldn't believe it. She'd just been to her first wedding and next week she was going to a birthday party with all her friends. *And* Aunt Violet had agreed to help her find the perfect presents for Angus and Uncle Digby.

THE
SEARCH

Clementine and Aunt Violet put on their coats and headed out into the afternoon sunshine. When Clemmie had asked Lavender if she wanted to go for a walk, the little pig had rolled over and kept her eyes firmly closed. Pharaoh was asleep too. He slept a lot.

Loud music filled the garden and Clementine wanted to stop and have another peek at what was happening. She and Aunt Violet poked their heads inside the marquee and laughed

when they saw Uncle Orville on the dance floor copying the moves of some beautiful young women in saris.

'Silly old fool,' Aunt Violet huffed.

Clementine giggled.

Mr Smote was standing near the entrance and overseeing the celebration when he noticed Aunt Violet and Clementine. He shuffled over beside them. 'It's all going beautifully,' he said happily. 'I think we could definitely recommend Penberthy House for more weddings.'

'That's wonderful,' Clementine replied. 'Mummy will be so pleased, won't she, Aunt Violet?'

Aunt Violet looked as if she had trodden in something smelly. 'I suppose so.'

The pair said goodbye to Mr Smote and continued through the field at the back of the garden, across the stone bridge and past the church to the Moggs' shop.

'Do you know what you're looking for, Clementine?' her great-aunt asked as they made their way inside.

Clementine shook her head. She hadn't a clue, but thought she might know when she saw it.

Unfortunately, Mrs Mogg's range of toys was rather small and hardly any were suitable for Angus. Clementine searched and searched but nothing was right.

When it came to finding something for Uncle Digby, she considered several options. He liked aftershave, but she knew that he only wore a certain kind. A new pen could be nice, but there were only plain ones. At last Clementine remembered that he liked to play cards, but she couldn't find any. Mr Mogg said that Father Bob had bought the last set earlier in the day.

This was turning out to be much harder than Clemmie had thought.

'Why don't you just make Pertwhistle a card and be done with it?' Aunt Violet suggested.

Clementine supposed she could do that, but it still didn't solve the problem of finding something for Angus.

'Your mother might be able to get something tomorrow over at Highton Mill,' her great-aunt said. 'Or, even better, doesn't she have a present cupboard at home?'

Clementine nodded. Of course she did. Why hadn't she thought of that earlier? Her mother had won so many things over the years that she had a whole cupboard full of bits and pieces. Surely Clemmie could find something in there.

Clementine and Aunt Violet said goodbye to Mr Mogg, who seemed very happy to see them go. It probably had something to do with the sound of football on the television out the back. On the way home, Clementine stopped several times to pick up coloured leaves, which she thought she could use to decorate her card for Uncle Digby.

Clementine was leaning down beside the stone wall when she jumped back in surprise. There was something wedged in the wall.

'Aunt Violet,' she called. 'Come and look at this.'

Her great-aunt sniffed and sauntered over.

'What's that?' Clementine pointed at the wall.

Aunt Violet peered into the space. 'My goodness. I haven't seen one of those in years. Not since I was a girl.' She reached in and carefully pulled out the strange object.

Clementine looked at her wide-eyed. 'Does it bite?' she asked.

Aunt Violet laughed. 'No, Clementine, of course not.'

Clementine had never seen anything so beautiful. 'It's lovely.'

'Yes, and very rare too, I think. I seem to recall Pertwhistle having a collection of these when he first came to work at the house.'

'Really?' Clementine asked.

'Yes. He kept them on the windowsill in the kitchen.'

'Do you think he'd like it?' Clementine asked.

'I suspect it would be perfect,' Aunt Violet said with a nod. 'It's very fragile, Clementine. Why don't we take it home and wrap it up safely?'

Clementine agreed. Now she just had to find the perfect present for Angus too.

PEACE
AND QUIET

Lady Clarissa was thrilled with Clementine and Aunt Violet's find. She located a box and helped Clementine wrap it carefully. A quick search through the present cupboard revealed many treasures a little boy would love. Clementine found something she thought would be just right and her mother helped her wrap it as well.

'Why don't you make the cards for Uncle Digby and Angus?' her mother suggested. 'Then we can tape them to the boxes and make sure they don't get mixed up.'

Lady Clarissa frowned. She probably should have found some different wrapping paper for each present but that was the one thing she'd been running low on.

Early in the evening, Mrs Fox appeared at the kitchen door. Aunt Violet and Clementine were at the table reading together and Lady Clarissa was busy getting the household's dinner ready. She was wondering how late the festivities in the garden would continue.

'Ahem,' said Mrs Fox.

Lady Clarissa stopped chopping the carrots and turned around. 'Oh, hello. Please come in.'

'I'd just like to give you this.' Mrs Fox held out an envelope.

'Is the wedding over?' Clarissa asked.

'Yes, Harriet and Ryan left a few minutes ago and we're about to pack up and head home too,' Mrs Fox said.

'I hope it all went well?' Lady Clarissa felt a little scared to ask. Mrs Fox hadn't been the easiest of house guests.

Mrs Fox beamed. 'Marvellous. Hector and

I couldn't have been more thrilled. The food was stunning, the setting was beautiful and Mr Smote – well, the man's a magician.'

Clementine smiled to herself. She knew that already.

'I'm so glad you've had a good day,' Lady Clarissa said with a relieved smile. 'And I'm sorry about not being here when you arrived.'

'Don't worry yourself about that,' Mrs Fox tutted. 'I just hope that Mr Pertwhistle is better soon. Heaven knows we *all* have our challenges with the elderly.'

Aunt Violet frowned.

'Uncle Orville, of course,' Mrs Fox said quickly.

'Oh, of course,' said Aunt Violet, nodding.

Lady Clarissa took the envelope and put it on the sideboard. She rather hoped its contents might cover the new roof. 'I'll see you off then.' She led Mrs Fox to the front hall.

Clementine followed, and bumped into Dr Gunalingam at the bottom of the stairs. He was bringing down the last of his family's bags.

'Goodbye, Clementine,' the man said. 'It was lovely to meet you.'

'Have the children gone already?' Clementine asked. She was hoping to say goodbye to Arya, Alisha and Aksara. 'They're all sound asleep in the car, I'm afraid. And Clemmie –' Dr Gunalingam looked at her seriously – 'I'm sure that Mr Pertwhistle will be fine.'

Clementine beamed. 'Thank you. Please say goodbye to Mrs Gunalingam and the children from me.'

Clementine joined her mother at the front door. As the Gunalingams' and the Foxes' cars drove away, she turned to her mother.

'Can you help me find my princess dress?' she asked.

'Of course, darling. And I have a surprise for you too.'

Clementine looked up at her mother. 'A surprise?'

'Yes, the hospital called a little while ago. Uncle Digby should be home on Tuesday.'

Clementine beamed.

PERFECT

Clementine couldn't wait to tell her friends that she was going to Angus's party too. Her mother had telephoned Mrs Archibald on Sunday afternoon to apologise for their very late RSVP and explained the mix-up with the mail. Mrs Archibald told Clarissa that Angus had been sad that Clementine wasn't coming to his party, but he'd be very happy now.

Clementine wondered if that was true or if Mrs Archibald had just said it to be kind.

But when she got to school, Angus ran straight up to her.

'I'm glad you're coming to my party,' he said, grinning.

'Thank you, Angus,' Clementine replied.

'Yeah, 'cos now my dragon will have something tasty to eat.'

Poppy rolled her eyes at him. 'You don't even have a dragon.'

'Yes, I do, and it eats girls,' Angus said and pulled a face. 'But it only likes sweet ones so that means it won't eat you, Poppy.'

Clementine leapt to her friend's defence. 'That's not very nice, Angus! But at least it won't eat me either.'

'Yes it will,' Angus insisted.

Joshua had been standing beside Angus the whole time, and now he gave his friend a funny look. 'Do you *like* her?' he asked.

'No way!' Angus shook his head. 'She's a girl and I don't like any girls.' Angus ran off into the playground with Joshua hot on his heels.

Astrid walked over to Poppy and Clementine. 'Angus *does* like you,' she said.

Clementine was confused by this comment. 'I don't think so. He's always so mean to me.'

'It's a boy thing,' Astrid explained. 'They're always mean to girls they like, so he probably likes you too, Poppy.'

Poppy pulled a face. 'Well, I don't like *him*, that's for sure.'

'I don't understand boys,' Clementine said seriously. But she was glad that Astrid did.

The day seemed to go by in a blink. Lady Clarissa picked Clementine up after school and when they got home the marquee was gone and there was hardly anything to remind Clemmie of the excitement of the weekend.

That evening, her mother helped pack her princess costume into a separate bag along with Angus's present, which Clementine took from the sideboard in the kitchen where it had been sitting next to Uncle Digby's.

Clementine took ages to fall asleep. She was so excited about the party and she couldn't wait for Uncle Digby to get home either.

Unlike Monday, Tuesday seemed to drag on forever. Mrs Bottomley got cross with the children asking her what time it was over and over. She decided she might as well use their interest to have some lessons on reading a clock. Clementine thought that was long overdue. She'd been wanting to learn to tell the time ever since the first day.

When the bell finally rang, Mrs Bottomley supervised the children getting changed into their costumes. Much to Clementine's distaste, Mrs Bottomley made them form two straight lines to march the short distance to Angus's house. It was only around the corner from the school. They must have looked a strange lot in their crowns and robes, especially the children who were brandishing swords and sceptres.

The group was ushered out into the back garden.

'Hello Mr Smote,' Clementine cried, as she ran up to the man. He too was dressed as a king.

'Clementine!' He made a deep bow. 'How lovely to see you again.'

She glanced around the garden and saw a huge cardboard castle. It was big enough for the children to clamber into. There were shields hanging from the fence and even some wooden horses for the guests to be photographed riding.

'You really are a magician!' Clementine said.

'It was nothing much,' the man replied modestly. 'And Angus is such a good boy.'

Mr Smote definitely hadn't seen Angus at school, Clementine thought to herself.

Angus's mother and Mr Smote had arranged lots of games for the children to play. There was pass the parcel and pin the tail on the pony, musical statues and hide and seek. Clementine and her friends weren't as keen on that one, as Angus kept pointing out where he kept his dragon.

Astrid marched off to the bottom of the garden and hid right where Angus said the dragon had its lair. Clementine thought she was terribly brave.

The afternoon went very quickly. As the sun started to fade, Angus blew out the candles on his castle cake and the children gathered around to watch him open his presents. Some of the parents had started to arrive too.

Joshua had bought him a train set, Poppy had given him a superhero dress-up costume and Sophie gave him a football.

Clementine's present was last of all. She and her mother had found him a tiny remote-controlled bug that could actually fly. Clementine would like to have kept it for herself but her mother said that it would make a lovely gift for a six-year-old boy.

The children stood around watching and waiting as Angus tore open the paper. Clementine looked at the little brown box. Her heart sank.

Angus pulled off the lid and stared. For a moment he didn't say a thing. Clementine was about to speak but Angus got in first.

'Wow!' he gasped. 'That's the best present ever.'

Clementine gulped. 'But it's the wrong one.'

'What do you mean?' Angus looked at her with a frown.

'That's not yours.' Clementine's lip trembled and tears prickled the backs of her eyes.

'But it's cool,' Angus said, 'and it's mine now.' He gently lifted the shell from the box. 'Whoa, what is it?'

Mrs Bottomley leaned in and inspected the gift. 'That is a very rare and precious cicada shell,' she informed the wide-eyed onlookers.

'It's the best present ever.' Angus was so excited he turned and kissed Clementine's cheek.

Everyone giggled and Clemmie's cheeks flushed pink.

Angus's ears turned bright red.

'Gross! Girl germs,' Joshua called out.

A hand reached through the crowd and Mrs Tribble yanked her son by her side. She scooped him up and kissed him noisily on the cheek too. 'I'll give you girl germs, Joshua Tribble.'

Joshua's howls of protest had everyone in stitches.

'Don't worry, Clementine,' came a voice beside her. It was Aunt Violet. 'Pertwhistle will understand.'

Clemmie glanced up, surprised. She hadn't noticed her great-aunt arrive. 'Do you really think so?'

Aunt Violet winked. 'I know so.'

It was time to go. The children said goodbye and Angus handed out the lolly bags. When he gave Clementine hers he even said another special thankyou and gave her a hug. Clementine kept her hands by her side as he squeezed her extra tight.

'I love it,' Angus whispered.

'Come along, Clemmie,' her great-aunt instructed. 'Your mother and Uncle Digby should be home by now.'

'Uncle Digby,' Clementine yelled as she ran ahead of her great-aunt into the house. Uncle

Digby was sitting at the kitchen table sipping a cup of tea and looking his usual self again.

He grinned at her. 'Hello there, miss.'

Clementine raced around and gave the old man a tight squeeze. 'We missed you so much. And Mummy and Aunt Violet and Mrs Mogg had to run the whole wedding and it was almost a disaster when the hot water broke but then Aunt Violet fixed it,' she babbled. 'Is your heart better?'

'My old ticker is just fine. Nothing to worry about,' he replied.

She was glad to hear it. It seemed that Arya was right about her father being able to fix broken hearts.

Clementine released Uncle Digby and rushed over to the sideboard. Uncle Digby's card was there with Angus's present. She picked up the card and took it over to the table.

Aunt Violet motioned at the little box. 'Go on, Clementine, give Uncle Digby his present too,' she said.

'But . . .' Clementine began.

'But nothing, Clementine. It's the thought that counts,' her great-aunt encouraged her.

Clemmie raced back and picked up the parcel. She looked with sad eyes at the old man. 'I wanted this to be perfect.'

Uncle Digby studied the card. On the front was a picture of Clementine and Lavender standing beside Aunt Violet and Pharaoh and Lady Clarissa. It said: 'What's missing?'

He opened it up and inside there was a picture of himself.

'You', it said. A tear formed in the corner of his eye. He brushed it away hastily and then read the message aloud. Clementine had told her mother what she wanted to say and then copied it carefully into the card after her mother had written it on a piece of paper.

Dear Uncle Digby, get well soon. We miss you so much – even Aunt Violet. Lots of love, Clementine and Lavender xxx

Uncle Digby laughed. So did Lady Clarissa, and even Aunt Violet managed to smile.

'Well, aren't you going to open your present?' Aunt Violet asked.

Digby Pertwhistle picked at the sticky tape and then unwrapped the paper. Clementine stood beside him as he lifted the lid off the box.

'Oh!' he exclaimed. 'I've wanted one of these since I was a boy.'

'Really?' Clementine grinned. 'Is that true?'

Aunt Violet coughed. 'They didn't make them a hundred years ago, Pertwhistle.'

He pulled out the remote-controlled bug, which closely resembled a giant bumblebee, and the little controller that went with it.

'Let's give it a whirl.' He flicked the switch. The tiny wings began to flap. The insect took off, whizzing through the air and dive-bombing Aunt Violet.

'Steady on there, man,' she yelled.

His mouth twitched. 'Oh, we're going to have a lot of fun with this one.' He sent the bug flying past Lavender, who grunted loudly, and Pharaoh, who swatted at it with his paw.

'Thank you, Clementine. It's perfect.' Uncle

Digby put his arm around her and kissed the top of her head just as the little bug crash-landed onto the table, right into the middle of one of Pierre's strawberry sponge cakes.

Clementine gave Uncle Digby a hug and then smiled at her mother and great-aunt. Yes, it was – just perfect.

CAST OF
CHARACTERS

The Appleby household

Clementine Rose Appleby — Five-year-old daughter of Lady Clarissa

Lavender — Clemmie's teacup pig

Lady Clarissa Appleby — Clementine's mother and the owner of Penberthy House

Digby Pertwhistle — Butler at Penberthy House

Aunt Violet Appleby — Clementine's grandfather's sister

Pharaoh	Aunt Violet's beloved sphynx cat

Friends and village folk

Margaret Mogg	Owner of the Penberthy Floss village shop
Clyde Mogg	Husband of Mrs Mogg
Father Bob	Village minister
Pierre Rousseau	Owner of Pierre's Patisserie in Highton Mill

School staff and students

Miss Arabella Critchley	Head teacher at Ellery Prep
Mrs Ethel Bottomley	Teacher at Ellery Prep
Sophie Rousseau	Clementine's best friend – also five years old
Poppy Bauer	Clementine's good friend – also five years old
Angus Archibald	Naughty kindergarten boy
Joshua Tribble	Friend of Angus's
Astrid	Clever kindergarten girl

Others

Mrs Tribble	Joshua's mother
Sebastian Smote	Wedding planner
Dr Brendan Gunalingam	Groom's brother
Karthika Gunalingam	Groom's sister-in-law
Arya, Alisha and Aksara Gunalingam	Groom's nieces and nephew
Ryan Gunalingam	Groom
Harriet Fox	Bride
Roberta and Hector Fox	Bride's parents
Uncle Orville Fox	Great-uncle of the bride

ABOUT THE AUTHOR

Jacqueline Harvey taught for many years in girls' boarding schools. She is the author of the bestselling Alice-Miranda series and the Clementine Rose series, and was awarded Honour Book in the 2006 Australian CBC Awards for her picture book *The Sound of the Sea*. She now writes full-time and is working on more Alice-Miranda and Clementine Rose adventures.

www.jacquelineharvey.com.au

JACQUELINE
SUPPORTS

Jacqueline Harvey is a passionate educator who enjoys sharing her love of reading and writing with children and adults alike. She is an ambassador for Dymocks Children's Charities and Room to Read. Find out more at www.dcc.gofundraise.com.au and www.roomtoread.org.